Twice Bitten

Twice Bitten

Gerald Hammond

St. Martin's Minotaur
New York

ISBN 0-312-24256-5

First published in Great Britain by Macmillan, an imprint of Macmillan Publishers Ltd

First U.S. Edition: December 1999

10 9 8 7 6 5 4 3 2 1

I am grateful to Alan Wood of the United Kingdom Blade Association, Mr Wilson of Wilson and Sons (Dundee) Ltd., dog-food manufacturers, and to Keith Erlandson, the gun dog guru, for patiently answering a lot of daft questions.

Preface

It was cold on the hill, and all the colder for what we had just found. The body itself was warmer than we were by far, but it had been roasted as if for some cannibal meal. I had smelled burnt bodies before, in the Falklands and elsewhere, and it was always shocking, not by virtue of what it was and certainly not because the smell itself was bad, but because it smelled like any other roasting meat.

But this was all the worse because I thought that I knew who it was.

The crime had grown from seeds planted years earlier, although I could not have known it at the time. I say 'the crime', but in my opinion there were two crimes and the one recognized by the law was the lesser.

Our involvement had begun more than a year before . . .

Chapter One

I remember the night early that spring when Mim was born. The occasion stands out from all the other births which have now rather merged together in my memory, only the latest whelping ever being distinct in my mind. We have had rather a lot of springer spaniel and other litters at Three Oaks Kennels over the years.

Either Daffy or Hannah (our two kennel-maids) would normally attend a whelping. Bitches can usually manage very well on their own and when one of them beats the calendar and fools us she can be counted on to show us a perfect litter with pride next morning. (Puppies, like babies, are nearly always born in the small hours.) So we have never made a rule about it, but the girls are conscientious and involved and they share the duty of attending the *accouchement* according to a roster of their own devising. If there is any reason to expect a problem, Isobel, a partner and a qualified vet, will keep the sitter-up company or be available 'on call'. But this was not Hebe's first litter and no trouble was foreseen.

On this occasion Rex, Daffy's husband, was away

3

on the oil rig so when Hebe was seen to be moving restlessly and making a nest for herself, Daffy dozed in the armchair in the heated whelping shed. All went well. Daffy even managed a few hours of sleep and had been home for a shower and change. Isobel, who had expressed every confidence in the outcome, was as anxious as anybody and arrived in a rush long before her usual time, just as Beth and I descended the stairs in the old farmhouse and deposited Sam on top of the two cushions on his chair in the big kitchen. Beth and Daffy set about making breakfast. Beth whipped up something special for Sam and, to his indignation, Isobel started spooning it into him. There are no lines of demarcation at Three Oaks Kennels.

'How did it go?' Beth asked Daffy.

'Seven,' Daffy said. 'All thriving.'

Isobel picked up immediately on the reserve in Daffy's voice and flashed her pink-framed spectacles at the younger woman. 'You don't sound very sure,' she said.

'One of them looks slightly odd.'

That was enough for Isobel. The occasional still-born pup could be accepted, but oddities might indicate a genetic freak affecting the whole of our carefully sculptured breeding line. She left Sam to feed himself, which he was quite capable of doing with only occasional lapses, and was out of the house like a whippet. She was well into her fifties but if anything was wrong with one of the dogs she could show a remarkable turn of speed. A quick flash of sunshine, a slam of the door and she was gone.

'Look who's talking,' Beth said.

Daffy looked up from the frying pan and put out her tongue. This, bearing in mind that Beth is the third partner, was a piece of impertinence. Daffy also shook her head. I was mildly disappointed to see that although she was still as always an eccentric dresser she had given up wearing a violently coloured stripe in her hair. I had rather enjoyed the daily changing splash of colour. 'There's nothing much wrong with her,' she said plaintively. 'Or nothing very much. I only said that she looks slightly odd.'

'She,' Beth said. 'Damn!' Bitch pups, as well as commanding a higher price, were essential to our breeding programme. 'What else have we got?'

'Three dogs, three bitches.'

'What do you mean, "odd"?' I asked Daffy.

'Nothing awful. Her ears are black, but the rest of her looks grey rather than black and white. And her face doesn't look quite right. The bitch couldn't have been served twice?'

'No,' I said. 'She couldn't.'

Hannah came in from feeding the other youngsters. Adhering rigidly to the job in hand, she had, with more restraint than the rest of us would have shown, passed by the whelping kennel without looking in on the new litter. Before we had finished explaining, Isobel returned, relief showing clearly on her homely face. 'Not to panic,' she said, brooding over Sam again. 'What we've got is a—'

The last word was lost to me in a splutter from the frying pan.

5

'A loony?' Daffy said doubtfully.

'A Clunie,' Isobel corrected. 'That's what they're commonly known as.' She looked round our faces. The two girls were frankly puzzled. Beth put a plate of bacon and eggs in front of me and waited for elucidation. I got on with my breakfast and tried to look as though I knew what Isobel was talking about. Sam made it clear that he could not have cared less and concentrated on the more important subject of breakfast. Isobel, who studies gun dog bloodlines so intensely that she knows them better than the lines on her own face, resumed in tones which might have been used by one explaining the mysteries of the universe to a class of four-year-olds. 'A throwback to Champion Clunie of Netherbrae. It's a very strong set of genes and when they come back together, which they do now and again, the result takes after her in both appearance and temperament. I warned you when you chose the sire, you may remember. He has Clunie for a great-great-grandam and Hebe has the same only one generation further back.'

Now that she mentioned it I remembered that Isobel had uttered a few cautionary words, but she had made the risk sound remote and she is inclined to prophesy doom whenever gun dog genetics is under discussion. 'Surely,' I said, 'if Clunie was a champion . . .'

'She was a very talented bitch,' Isobel said. 'Quite brilliant on her day, but temperamental. She was sort of brindled with small spots instead of the larger patches of the usual spaniel, so that she looked grey from a distance. And she had a slightly undershot jaw, just like this pup. Not the kind of appearance to attract an owner. And her temperament was both nervous and headstrong.'

'And those of her descendants who inherit her looks have her temperament as well?' I asked, hoping that Isobel might have changed her opinion within the last few minutes.

'In my experience, invariably.'

'Oh dear!' I said mildly. We tried to be very careful of our language now that Sam was not only articulate but approaching school age. He had developed an uncanny knack of singling out the rude word and then picking on the very occasion when we would least like to hear it repeated. But as the principal trainer in the firm I knew that a headstrong dog which was also of a nervous and sensitive disposition was a trainer's nightmare. Whatever one did would be wrong for one side or the other of its nature. 'I'll take a look as soon as I've finished my breakfast,' I said. 'In your opinion, what do we do?'

'You certainly don't invest time and money training her to work,' Isobel said. 'And you can't sell her as a pup for an owner to train without damaging our reputation for only breeding the best. I don't see anyone buying her for a pet. We'd better put her down – unless HM Government wants her for a sniffer dog. Clunie had one of the finest noses in the business.'

There was a moment of uncomfortable silence. None of us had the least compunction about putting down the old and sick; each of us, indeed, would have supported the legalization of euthanasia. But we hated to put down any creature only because it was unwanted.

'Put me down,' Sam said suddenly. He meant that he wanted to be helped down from the cushion which raised him to a convenient height for feeding.

'Don't think we haven't thought of it,' Beth said affectionately. She heaved up her first-born and set him on his feet.

'Please,' Daffy said, 'don't decide just yet. Let's see what she looks like when her eyes open. If you want a good home for her . . . I might take her. I've been wanting one to train on my own account.'

'My dear girl,' said Isobel, 'you don't know what you'd be taking on.'

'If she's going to have the same temperament as Clunie,' Daffy said stubbornly, 'and Clunie was made up to Champion—'

'By the great Harry Stimson,' Isobel said. 'One of the greatest trainers ever and while he was at the height of his career. You'd be walking a tightrope between being too harsh and too soft.'

'I could learn to walk a tightrope,' Daffy said. 'Couldn't I?' she added in my direction.

Sam was dashing round and round the table, tooting in imitation of an Intercity train. It made rational thinking difficult but I tried very hard. Strictly, the duties of the two kennel-maids were concerned with feeding, cleaning, grooming and exercising our stock and the occupants of the boarding and quarantine kennels. But training followed by success in competition brought in both revenue and reputation. The girls, and Daffy in particular, had been expected to play with and 'humanize' the young pups. Daffy had also undertaken much of the elementary training. She had helped me by throwing dummies and firing blank cartridges during more advanced lessons. I had found that she had learned by watching, so that I could tell her to 'Go and give so-and-so a lesson with the dummy launcher', and know that it would be done with skill and sensitivity.

I had never dared to say so aloud, but I had rather hoped that when Isobel, who was the oldest of us three partners, retired from doing most of the handling in field trials, Daffy might be ready to take over. Since the illness which had ended my army career, I had remained subject to occasional fainting attacks that the doctors put down to vagal inhibition, in addition to which I had neither the stamina nor the steadfastness needed for consistent success in competition, both of which qualities Isobel had in plenty and Daffy seemed to be developing. A dog of her own might be the spur to further progress, and the more difficult the dog the further might be the progress. I could see a definite advantage in Daffy learning such lessons from mistakes made on her own dog rather than on one of the firm's.

'You've been coming on,' I said cautiously. 'But you still have a lot to learn.'

'You can teach me,' Daffy said. She caught Sam on his next circuit, sat him on her knee and popped a piece of toast into his mouth.

I was about to object to this bland assumption that I would spend my valuable time and energy on training a possible future rival in the field, when Beth chipped in. 'Let her try,' she said. 'We owe Daffy a lot.'

'I've no objection,' Isobel said, 'provided, first, that she doesn't carry our kennel-name and second, that she's never bred from.'

Probably they were both influenced by the blissful but temporary silence. Daffy, however, seized the moment. 'That's agreed, then,' she said, transferring Sam to Isobel's knee. 'Work to be done. Come on, Hannah.' She headed out of the room before anybody could think of any counter-arguments.

The pup was named Mimulus – Mim for short, although there had already been a Mimosa. At eight weeks, she was removed and ownership transferred to Daffy. But we soon began to see a lot of her. Rex, Daffy's husband, was often to be seen leading the fast-growing pup around on a plaited leather leash, but when Rex was offshore (two weeks out of four) Mim came to Three Oaks with Daffy and mingled with our dogs.

For half a year, all went well. Love and patience seemed to be achieving what conventional wisdom could not. Mim learned to sit, stay, come, lie down and walk reliably at heel. She made progress at retrieving dummies. I was adamant that she must not be introduced to retrieving real game too early – that way lies the mortal sin of running-in – but she learned to retrieve dummies decorated with pheasant wings or rabbit skins by marking, memory, hand signals or scenting.

Sam also was learning. The first and most essential lesson for a child around a kennels was not to provoke a dog into biting him. One sharp nip taught him sense without, I was pleased to see, giving him any real fear. The second was to wash thoroughly after mingling with the dogs and before touching food or his face. Once those two lessons had been ingrained he was free to visit the dogs, admire the young pups or help the girls with the chores. Young children can sometimes develop a better rapport with dogs than their elders. A dog has little reasoning power but a child, even one who would be going to school in a year or so, not being particularly well furnished in that direction, does not expect it. Sam took a particular fancy to Mim. Daffy insisted that without his company as playmate and assistant trainer, Mim would never have made the progress that she did.

One of Mim's admirers was Quentin Cove. Quentin owned a large farm over to the west of Cupar. He lived alone but he was a sociable man, a back-slapper with a loud laugh and a huge appetite for food and drink and, it was said, despite his bachelor status, women. I got on well enough with him although Beth usually managed to avoid him. Like many Scotsmen of rural upbringing but good education, he was well spoken but inclined to lapse into the Scots tongue when excited.

When the economic climate and the Government between them turned against farming, Quentin had decided to diversify. He was the third generation of Coves to own Ardrossie, so capital was not in short supply. Some lightweight, modern buildings had been erected on a corner of his land and he had set up as a manufacturer and supplier of dog-food. He was adamant that the move arose from no more than sound economics, but I suspected that he had had in mind the interests of his farm-workers who were being displaced by advancing technology. The day-to-day management of the farm was left to his farm manager, Dougal Webb, a graduate from agricultural college but not too proud to drive a tractor or handle a shovel.

We made Quentin's acquaintance soon after our arrival at Three Oaks. He was newly started in the dog-food business at the time and was acting as his own sales manager. He called to see me, offering an unusual deal which had already been turned down by several of our more established rivals. Although, as a shooting man himself, he kept several dogs, he needed greater feedback than he could manage from his own resources. If we would keep daily records of how our dogs thrived on his products and also allow the use of our competition successes in his advertising, he would supply us with his dog-food at half price, without limit of time.

The offer seemed almost too good to be true. After a trial period, which proved to my and even Isobel's satisfaction that Quentin's product was as good as any and better than most, I jumped at it. At the factory the various mixtures were compressed into small and easily crumbled cakes of exact bulk, so that it was easy to count out the proper diet for a dog of any size and energy need. At first, Quentin was also his own delivery driver. Later, as his business grew, he employed others to drive his vans although most often our supplies were brought by Dougal Webb. The dog-food business was, strictly speaking, nothing to do with Dougal, but he was courting Hannah at the time and glad of the excuse to call.

During the summer Quentin, on one of his visits, met Daffy with Mim in the drive. He was very much taken with the spaniel, which was not surprising. Mim was becoming a very charming little dog. She had developed a habit, when Daffy held out her hand at hip level, of rearing up on her hind legs and thrusting her head against the hand, thus obtaining a pat without putting her mistress to any trouble. He enquired as to her pedigree and seemed very knowledgeable about Clunie of Netherbrae, which was not particularly sur-prising; Quentin's dogs were cousins to our stock. He told Daffy that if she ever wanted to part with Mim she could expect a good offer. Daffy said that Mim was a champion of the future and advised him not to hold his breath.

Mim's progress was too good to last.

One morning, at Daffy's home beyond the village and only a few days after Quentin's visit, a metal basin which Daffy was taking down from a high shelf slipped from her fingers. The noise, she said later, was just as she imagined a bomb would sound and, by mischance, the basin landed beside the sleeping Mim and caught the spaniel a crack over the nose as it bounced.

The effect on a nervous young dog may be imagined. Poor Mim developed a fear of loud noises which was resistant to normal treatments. In vain we fed her titbits while hands were gently clapped at varying distances. It took only the sound of a carelessly closed door to send her into the shelter of the nearest pair of friendly legs.

Worse was to follow. One week later, Rex was walking with Mim in farmland on the other side of the village. The spaniel seemed to be in better spirits and was quartering the grass, picking up scents and, no doubt, wondering what they might foretell. They reached a crest crowned by gorse bushes. Drawn by the scent of rabbits, Mim pushed into the cover.

Nobody can be quite sure what happened next, but it seems that the farmer was also looking for rabbits, but on the far side of the bushes. He saw a rabbit. There are rabbit holes just there and bunny probably went to ground. But the farmer saw a grey shape flitting through the bushes, which was almost certainly Mim. Whatever the explanation, Mim heard the sound of a shot and collected about a dozen pellets of Number Six shot.

The farmer was as horrified as Mim and Rex. He Land Rovered them straight to us at Three Oaks. While Isobel Kitts struggled to remove any pellets which were in danger of aggravating the physical damage, Rex sat with his head in his hands and told the story.

'What put the bloody lid on it for me,' he finished, 'was that when we reached the road and were lifting her into the Land Rover, Sanctimonious Pratt drove by. And he wagged a finger at us. He must have thought that one of us had run the dog over.'

I was duly sympathetic. Timothy Pratt, a freelance photographer and cameraman, was well known locally. He was often nicknamed 'Sanctimonious' because of his habit of sermonizing over anyone who he had at a moral disadvantage. He had political ambitions and by strange chance often figured heroically on television in his own film clips. At the moment he was admired without being liked. Millions of viewers had seen him attempting to rescue an injured motorcyclist and being himself burned in the attempt. Whatever characteristics Sanctimonious Pratt might lack, courage was not one of them; but it must have been gall and wormwood to Rex to be admonished by him at such a time and from a safe distance.

Isobel managed to tidy Mim up without serious harm, but the damage to Mim's morale could never be repaired and I was forced to agree that she was now totally and incurably gun-shy.

Daffy, as far as I know, never reproached Rex, but Rex never forgave himself. Daffy was heartbroken. She loved Mim but she had set her heart on bringing a pup of her own to field trial standard. A chronically gun-shy dog would be a total loss for trials and might very well pass on her nervousness to any kennel-mate. Very reluctantly, Daffy and Rex agreed that Mim would have to go.

Daffy approached Quentin Cove and, although she was perfectly honest about the gun-shyness, received an acceptable offer. Mim was handed over. Daffy was subdued and occasionally tearful for several days but eventually another puppy which Rex, nobly abandoning for the moment his intention of building a sports car from a kit, insisted was properly bought and paid for this time, took her mind off Mim although she never forgot some of the lessons she had learned. They named the new puppy Sarda – the acronym of the Search and Rescue Dogs Association although, as Isobel pointed out more than once, the name would have more properly suited a Labrador.

For the moment, all seemed well.

The critical stage in the training of any dog which is to compete in field trials or be sold as a working gun dog is the introduction to live quarry. For this purpose, rabbits are useful and sometimes essential. The dog may have been schooled in all the basic skills, will have learned to quarter the ground, to obey whistles and hand signals, to ignore rabbits in the rabbit pen and to retrieve cold game. It may even have learned the futility of chasing after an airborne pheasant. But a running rabbit is an open invitation to chase. Perhaps the biggest hurdle in training is for the dog to learn to hunt the rabbit out of cover and then to stop dead, just when temptation is at its strongest, until sent for the retrieve. Happily for the dog trainer, most farmers regard the rabbit much as a fond mother regards the common nit. A shooter with a dog, both of whom can be trusted to respect crops and livestock, is usually welcomed.

That year, myxomatosis broke out again in our neighbourhood. It was not as total as in previous years – the infection is carried by the rabbit flea, which is mostly transferred in tightly occupied burrows, but rabbits now live more above-ground than they used to. And rabbits have developed a resistance to the virus. It was becoming quite common to gather a healthy rabbit with old mixy scars around the eyes. But those bunnies that caught the infection were seriously ill while it lasted. The disease was not communicable to dogs, but rabbits which hopped slowly or sat still were going to teach the dogs nothing that I wanted them to know and much that I hoped they would never find out.

Late that summer, Dougal Webb made the regular run with a supply of dog-food. He was a thickset young man with black, curly hair, a round and ruddy face and a square jaw. Beth and I both felt, for reasons that we could not put into words, that he was not a man for a young girl, or anybody else, to trust. He was just a little too sure of his welcome, too pleased with himself and certain that his allure would have the desired effect. For Hannah, it did just that. As far as she was concerned, the sun shone out of his every orifice. She could hardly utter a coherent word while he was around. Beth said that this was because he brought with him his own cloud of pheromones and testosterone and God alone knew what else. I couldn't see it myself. Dougal Webb also had a taste for life's more luxurious capital goods. I put forward the theory that free spending on a man's part might be a more powerful aphrodisiac than a whole cloud of personal chemicals. Beth, who was out of patience with me at the time, said that she wouldn't know about that, never having experienced either of them.

Dougal Webb was certainly a free spender though more, as far as I could judge, on his own comforts and status than on his lady friends. He dressed well and ran around in a Lotus quite unsuited to life on a farm. He wore a Rolex watch which I frankly envied. At first glance I had supposed it to be a fake, but the movement of the second hand confirmed that it was the genuine article. I had only once seen a similar model, and that had been on the wrist of one of the local landowners.

Although Dougal was devoted to expensive possessions, he was remarkably thrifty about little things. The abhorrence of waste which had probably endeared him to Quentin as a farm manager extended even to finishing every last crumb on his plate, so although Dougal once explained his lifestyle with a passing reference to a legacy, I guessed that he had known hard times. His visit was timed, as usual, to suit an invitation to the snack which passes with us for lunch, but whether this was due to thrift or lust was uncertain.

For once, nobody was away competing or engaged in some task too urgent to be left. We all managed to sit down together, so that the table in the big kitchen was crowded around and almost covered with crockery. In addition to Dougal, Sam and the five members of the firm, Henry, Isobel's husband, had walked over to join us, as was his frequent habit.

The myxomatosis that was still rife around Three Oaks had struck earlier further south and passed on, leaving a slightly reduced but still thriving population behind. Sam, who was passing through a garrulous phase – or so we hoped – had been almost monopoliz ing the conversation but I seized on a moment when his mouth was full. 'I need to do some training on rabbits within the next day or two,' I told Dougal. 'Will it be all right if I come and work two or three dogs through your set-aside land?'

Dougal swallowed quickly. 'I'm afraid not,' he said. 'Mr Cove tells me that he's let the rough shooting over the farm, so he doesn't feel that he can let anybody else on. It wasn't any of my doing,' he added in what seemed to be genuine apology.

'I understand,' I said.

The loss of access to one farm was not a serious blow. I had been cultivating farmers for a long time, always asking each for an introduction and recommendation to his neighbours. Although it meant a big outlay on thank-you bottles at Christmas, at least I was never without land to train on. But Henry may have thought that either Dougal or I would appreciate a quick change of subject, because he suddenly asked Dougal, 'How's Quentin getting on with Mim?'

This subject was more sensitive than the other. Hannah was looking at Dougal as though he had been handing down tablets of stone, but I saw Daffy and Sam exchange a look of sadness. Spaniels are very loving little dogs. Once in a while one meets up with one of their number which is exceptionally both loving and giving. Sarda, Mim's replacement, was one of these; but Mim had had a special place in Daffy's heart and Sam's.

Dougal shrugged. 'That's the spotted one? I don't have much to do with the dogs. I believe he's very pleased with her.'

'Is he managing to do anything about the gun-shyness?' Henry persisted.

'He hasn't said anything, but I saw him working her with the dummy launcher the other day. I don't think he can be having too much trouble.'

I saw Daffy bite her lip. I knew that she was thinking that I was a false prophet. Perhaps, if she had persevered . . .

After lunch, I caught Daffy on her own. 'Don't blame yourself,' I said, 'or me. If he's had any success with the gun-shyness it may have been at the expense of something else. And even if Mim becomes a Dual Champion, it doesn't follow that you could have achieved the same. Just be happy for her.'

'You're probably right,' Daffy said. But I could see that she did not believe it.

Chapter Two

Soon after that, autumn came round again, the shooting season opened and we were too busy to think about Quentin Cove. My own shooting engagements were infrequent, but I was picking-up several times in most weeks. The job of the pickers-up is to observe from behind the standing Guns and to use their dogs to collect any fallen birds other than those gathered by the Guns themselves. The opportunity is not to be missed, offering the trainer the ideal chance to give his dogs a final polish while at the same time having to himself the most enjoyable part of the day's sport and even being paid for it – albeit a comparative pittance. Trustworthy handlers and dogs are in demand by shoot organizers, to put birds in the bag and to give a merciful end to any not killed outright by the shot.

Along with shooting season, the season of field trials came rushing at us. Keeping our name before the shooting public and a series of field trial champions in our dogs' pedigrees was the only way to convince the shooting man that one of our stock would be a more dependable purchase than the untried progeny of the bitch next door. Isobel, who had a remarkable talent and temperament for handling dogs under competition conditions, was competing almost every weekend. This, unfortunately, tied up at least one other member of the firm, because Isobel, who had a very poor head for those inevitable celebratory drinks, had succumbed once too often to temptation and had lost her driving licence – to the general relief because, even sober, she had been the sort of driver who causes other motorists to wake up in the small hours, gibbering.

It was my responsibility to bring the dogs through the successive stages of training and to send them off with Isobel as prepared as they could be to acquit themselves well in competition. At the same time, it was necessary for the other dogs which I was training to sell as workers, the guests in boarding and the virtual prisoners in the quarantine kennels to be fed and watered, cleaned and groomed and, with the exception of those in quarantine who had to make do with an illicit period of chasing a ball in the quarantine courtyard, walked. And during all this activity it was inevitable that any brood bitch who had failed to conceive in the spring and was now in an interesting condition would pick the most frantically inconvenient moment to produce her litter.

During the occasional brief intervals in this frenetic activity, we were much too tired to give more than a passing thought to absent friends. It was not until late October that Mim was brought to our notice again. By then, the first rush of activity on the grouse moors was over and estates were giving that year's pheasants a little more time to mature, so that there was a comparative lull. My picking-up engagements were at a standstill, but I had three dogs to prepare for imminent competitions. The local rabbit population was still very low and unlikely to increase until spring. One of my favourite farms had been heavily poached by ferreters and another had received its annual visit from a team who shot at night by lamp from the back of a Land Rover. I was driven to try some of the farms where active game-shooting took place but, as I feared, I would not be welcome at that time of year. As a next-to-last resort I phoned Alec Hatton.

Alec's farm, Lincraigs, lay between Ardrossie, Quentin Cove's farm, and Marksmuir, the wide-spread estate of Sir Ian Bewlay. Without compromising on the efficiency of his farming, Alec ran a small shoot with a syndicate of middle-income executives mostly from Glenrothes. He managed the shoot very well and at a modest subscription, by making use of volunteer labour from among his members, tucking small patches of game crops into every otherwise unusable corner of his land, releasing a modest number of pheasant poults and depending on an inward migration of birds from the much larger numbers reared and released for the commercial shooting on Marksmuir.

Alec hesitated. He was usually a generous man although he always managed to sound grudging. It was only a mannerism. 'The morn's morn?' he said. 'Aye. That'll be fine, if you'll go round and dog the bound aries. Turn my birds back, like. Speak to me after.'

Dog training with a gun is best not done solo. The act of shooting distracts from the dog handling and rabbits in particular are adept at breaking out of cover on the far side from the lone hunter. Beth always resisted my going off alone in case one of my blackouts overtook me while I was out of reach of ready help. Isobel, who would normally have come along to work the dogs while I used the gun, had seized on what would probably be the last quiet spell before February to take Henry away on a visit to a relative in Oban.

'Who's coming with me?' I asked the world in general.

Beth was usually willing to come along and to shoot, quite competently, while I got on with the training, but Sam had developed a cough. 'You go,' she told Daffy. 'Hannah and I can manage the chores.'

Daffy nodded happily.

In the morning, there was a thin covering of fresh snow, the first since the early spring, but the roads were passable. I had hardly slowed the car outside the cottage where she lived with Rex before Daffy was out of the door and running down the path. Sarda was too young to progress beyond obedience training and the retrieval of dummies but, with the prospect of her own dog to bring on for competitions, Daffy was as keen as any young pup to learn. In wellingtons and a full set of Barbours, she looked almost normal or perhaps even a member of the Establishment.

Twenty minutes later we passed Ardrossie Farm and the clutch of new buildings, dominated by silos and a square aluminium tower, out of keeping with the ancient countryside, where the dog-food was made.

As we bounced up the potholed farm-road to Lincraigs Alec Hatton, a distant figure on a tractor, waved to us.

Lincraigs Farm covered a large acreage and to dog the whole boundary would have taken more time than we could spare. But I could guess that it was the boundary with Marksmuir that concerned Alec. A farm track took us that way and I parked beside an enormous black-wrapped sausage of straw a hundred yards long. Evidently Alec was taking the fullest advantage of the new technology.

It was a marvellous day. Unexpected sunshine struck a sparkle from the snow without being warm enough to trigger a thaw. Beyond the boundary, Marksmuir was heavily wooded with beech and birch and rowan. On Lincraigs, tree strips and small copses had been preserved. A mild autumn had seen the leaves turn but they had not yet fallen. That first, light powdering of snow outlined the branches against a blue sky, and among the tracery the leaves glowed in the sunshine, gold and brown and orange and scarlet. It was a day to remember. Daffy had brought a camera for the sake of the dogs. An enlarged print of one of her shots hangs over my desk as I write. In the foreground, a rowan blazes with berries while beneath its branches a spaniel, with one paw raised and eyes alight, awaits the command, 'Get on!' The picture may be pretty rather than beautiful. It may belong on the lid of a chocolate-box. But it can still bring a glow to my heart.

But we were not there to enjoy the scenery. Daffy

put away the camera and took my gun from me. She was becoming a more than competent shot.

The snow made scenting difficult but it held a record of every creature that had set foot on it. In particular, it saved us wasting time hunting for rabbits where there were none. It also showed the arrowhead footprints of many pheasants. Most of them had been drawn over the boundary from Marksmuir into a long and narrow strip of kale along the boundary of Lincraigs and towards grain-filled feed-hoppers strategically placed among scattered gorse-bushes. The deliberate tempting of a neighbour's birds across the boundary was perfectly legal. It would have been generally denounced as un-neighbourly, but while Daffy knocked over the occasional rabbit, I worked the dogs, one at a time, with a clear conscience and sent pheasants onwards towards the two small woods at the heart of the Lincraigs shoot. Sir Ian Bewlay had never been among my favourite people and I was tickled by the thought of how the wandering would have infuriated his thrifty spirit.

In the cold air, sound travelled. On Gifford Hill, which humped up to the south of us, foresters were felling the conifer plantation, clearing the roots and waste branches by building the foundation for a huge future bonfire. In the process, a house was emerging where previously I had only seen a roof and chimneys. The sound of the foresters' voices came clearly between the bursts of chainsaw.

The spaniels seemed to be enjoying the beauty of the day. They worked with zest but stayed under control, making only occasional tries to test their handler's firmness as spaniels always will.

Between Lincraigs and Gifford Hill ran another back-road and where the boundary met the road stood a small but stoutly built cottage with a slated roof and walls of stone. The small garden was tidy but the flowers were over and the vegetables almost finished. I had seen the place before but never its occupant. That morning, as we reached the road a figure was entering the garden gate, a woman of around sixty. She was very small and even in her youth could never have been a beauty, having a flat nose, a disproportionately large mouth and a noticeable squint. The spaniel at work just then, Pru, being even more sociable than the rest, pushed through the hedge and went to make her acquaintance and she squeaked with delight and went down on her knees to pet the dog. (This was a breach of discipline on the part of Pru but it was too late to do anything much about it; the dog had already been rewarded with praise.)

She stood up, without becoming much taller, and came close to the hedge. 'Yon's gey bonny dogs you hae there,' she said. Although her speech was broad her voice was pure and she had a ready grin. Despite her goblinlike appearance, I found myself inclined to like her. Pru evidently agreed, because she reappeared at the woman's side bearing one of the rabbits that we had collected and delivered the limp body into her hands. The old woman accepted it without any sign of squeamishness. When she held it out to me I said, 'Keep it, if you'd like it.'

She smiled with the warmth that redeemed her face. 'I'd like it fine,' she said. 'Rabbit flesh is hailsome meat. I'm Elsie Dundee,' she added.

'John Cunningham.'

'I ken that,' she said. 'You're the dog man.'

I bade her a slightly cool farewell. I dislike being addressed as Captain but I once threatened to sue a journalist who referred to me as a dog man.

All went well until we were almost back at the car and ready to leave, when the youngest dog put up a cock pheasant which rocketed, gaudy in the sunshine, only to hit an overhead wire in a puff of bronze feathers and come spiralling down with a broken wing, just over the boundary. Burn, the oldest dog, brought it to me for the *coup de grâce*.

Even so early in the season, the game dealers were giving only the price of a pint of beer for a pheasant and this would soon be reduced to less than half. All the same, I was in no doubt that I must deliver the bird to Alec with an apology. One can feel totally alone in the countryside; but break a single rule and an observer will pop out of every bush. I turned the car and picked my way between the potholes back towards Lincraigs Farmhouse.

In the farmyard the tractor was muttering to itself like a bad-tempered old man, but at the farmhouse door Alec Hatton was talking to a visitor. As I stopped the car at the mouth of the yard they both looked round and I saw that the visitor was Dougal Webb, dressed for once not in his elegant casuals but in dusty jeans and a sweater. A few more quick words were exchanged before Dougal turned away. He gave us a cheerful nod as he went by. He vanished into a dip leading down through a field of set-aside land towards Ardrossie.

Alec Hatton followed more slowly. He was around forty, lightly built though I knew that he was very strong. I got out of the car to meet him, holding out the pheasant. 'You'd better take this,' I said.

He smiled to Daffy who was still in the car, then looked at me in surprise for several seconds. His weather-beaten face was as thin as his body and seemed have melted slightly so that his lower lip, his nose and even his eyelids seemed to droop despondently. He took the pheasant out of my hands and felt for the wing-tag. 'You mistook it for a flying rabbit?' he suggested.

'He flew into the overhead wires,' I explained.

He shook his head. 'I bet one of your dogs pegged it.'

This was almost fighting talk. For a trained dog to pick up an unpricked bird which was sitting tight would be an eliminating fault in a field trial and very close to being a cardinal sin. But I kept my temper. I had only lived in the area for seven or eight years, and it was quite customary for the native Fifer to needle one who would still be counted a stranger, just to test his reaction. 'You'd better pluck it for yourself,' I said patiently. 'You'll find a broken wing. And I wrung his neck. That's all. No shot. Do you want a dozen rabbits?'

My reply passed the test. He smiled suddenly, dissipating the apparent gloom of his features, and thrust the pheasant back at me. 'You keep it,' he said. 'Anyway, it's a Marksmuir bird, one of last year's from the tag. Yon mannie Cove might buy your rabbits.'

We both looked towards Ardrossie. The Lincraigs buildings were set on the edge of a rise overlooking the other farm. Below us, Dougal Webb had reached the boundary fence. I saw him put one hand on a fence post and vault nimbly over the barbed wire before unhesitatingly hopping the overhung ditch between two hawthorn trees. He seemed to be familiar with his way across. We could see over the corrugated roofs of the new buildings in their anodized, pastel colours to the sturdy old farm buildings. As we watched, Quentin Cove came out of the factory buildings and looked towards us, shading his eyes.

'I'll keep them,' I said. 'There's no point selling them cheap to him and then buying them back in his dogfood at three times the price. And I'll bet he's got plenty of rabbits on Ardrossie.'

Alec nodded. 'That's for sure,' he said. 'He'd likely be glad of a hand with them.'

'You'd think so,' I said. 'But he told young Dougal to tell me that he'd taken money for the rough shooting, so he couldn't in fairness give away permissions. Who would the shooting tenant be?'

Alec pushed back his cap and scratched a balding scalp. 'Dashed if I know. I've never seen a soul with a gun. Nor heard a shot since the last time you were over the ground a month or two back, except for Mr Cove hisself training his dogs. Are you and the lassie coming in for a fly cup?'

'We'll do that,' I said. Mrs Hatton's baking was the best for miles around, rivalled only by that of her two daughters. Also, you never know when some oddment of farming gossip may come in useful, if only as a topic of conversation.

The farmhouse kitchen was filled with delicious smells. There were fresh scones on the table and raspberry jam, and big mugs of tea. It was a comfortable haven after the crispness and activity of the morning.

Mrs Hatton was unashamedly stout. The two daughters were strapping girls who would probably go the same way as their mother in time. Alec Hatton had no employees but ran the farm with their help and making use of outside contractors. The girls were much in demand socially. Dorothy, the elder girl, we learned was engaged to be married to the son of a big farmer near Leslie. Her younger sister, Emily, was frankly envious. I hoped for Hannah's sake that Dougal Webb's visits to Lincraigs were business rather than pleasure. And yet, perhaps a jilting would not be the worst that could come to her. She was young enough to recover. We, on the other hand, might never find another such kennel-maid.

The topic of Dorothy's leaving the nest and its repercussions on the farm lasted until we were almost ready to leave. Then Daffy, who, with her own husband safely in the bag, had been listening with only half an ear, asked Alec, 'Do you see Mr Cove often, training his spaniels?'

'Most days, for an hour or so in the morn and again after his dinner. You can't help but see him,' Alec explained. 'If he's in a hurry, he just takes them onto the bittie rough ground at the end of the big barn. It's right under our noses, as you might say.'

'You said that you heard shots when he was training them.'

'That's right. He uses the gun, but I've seen him more often with the dummy thrower.'

'Have you seen him working with Mim? That's the brindled young bitch he got from us. But she'd look grey at a distance,' Daffy explained carefully.

Alec looked blank. His interest in dogs only extended as far as working collies and the dogs of his syndicate members. His daughters were the spaniel fanciers. Dorothy had a spaniel of Three Oaks breeding.

'I've seen her,' Dorothy said.

'Is she all right?' Daffy asked. 'Did she look happy and fit?'

'For all you can tell at a quarter-mile,' said Dorothy. 'She seemed to have plenty of energy.'

'Has he been complaining about gun-shyness?'

Alec laughed while eating cake and almost choked. 'We never discuss dogs with him these days. Not after the matter he made of it when Dorothy's dog covered one of his bitches.'

We got up to leave, but we were not to drive off straight away. Somebody had removed all four valves from the tyres of my car. Alec was very apologetic although the whole family had been in the kitchen with us when the deed was done. He set off immediately in his own car to obtain a set of valves from the nearest service station and then fetched a compressor from his tractor shed to re-inflate the tyres. We agreed that it must have been the work of small boys, with whom the area was over-provided.

Soon after that, life began to gather pace again.

Ash was entered in a novice stake for the Saturday. I was determined, as usual, to send him out with all his lessons fresh in his little mind. Familiarity with the 'real thing' is essential to a working dog's upbringing, but Ash was not short of experience picking-up. Conversely, to take him out on a solo expedition into the field would have been to risk a blank and wasted day. With a little ingenuity, all the basic lessons could be reinforced in the comfortably familiar atmosphere of home.

The snow had thawed, to be replaced by dull and sometimes drizzly weather. I had long before covered several dummies with pheasant skins. On the Friday morning, I fetched them out of the bag of fresh pheasant feathers in which, so that the scent would remain familiar, they were stored. In another field of set-aside land behind the house I set up several spring-operated devices of my own making which could toss a dummy, after the manner of a Roman ballista, in a reasonable mimicry of a rocketing pheasant. I fetched my gun, a blank adapter, some blank cartridges, Isobel and Henry, on the way out passing Dougal Webb who was making eyes at Hannah.

We spent a useful hour in the set-aside land. Isobel worked Ash to and fro, keeping him always under control. From time to time I would send up a dummy from one or another of my devices, Henry would fire a blank cartridge and the dummy would fall in the cover. When we were sure that Ash was steady and as closely in tune with his job as he ever would be, we knocked off before boredom could set in and undo the good work.

The trial was to be in Ayrshire. Isobel, chauffeured by Daffy, would have to set off that afternoon and make an overnight stay so, instead of going back to his kennel, Ash went into a travelling box in the back of my car.

The kitchen, containing both the range and the central-heating boiler, tends to overheat, so the back door often stands ajar. We found Dougal still leaning against the jamb in an attitude of calculated negligence, aiming flirtatious remarks at Hannah who, to do her justice, was concentrating on the preparation of a meal for the latest litter of pups. Dougal could seem almost dapper in his carefully chosen 'smart' gear, but today he was still in his dusty working clothes and looked almost ungainly.

Dougal, it seemed, was not so fixated on concupiscence as to forget other manly pursuits. He glanced round and stiffened like a pointer. 'Nice gun,' he said. 'May I look?' I was carrying one of my dummy traps in one hand. He took my Dickson Round Action from under my other arm without waiting for my permission, dropped the barrels and looked through at the daylight outside. The gesture proved nothing except that he knew how to operate the top-lever. With the blank cartridge adapters in place he could have seen very little. But he inspected the sparse engraving and tried the gun to his shoulder several times.

Hannah, noticeably piqued, was making little noises to attract his attention but was ignored in the face of more macho attractions. 'Very nice indeed,' Dougal said, closing and handing back the gun. 'I bet that cost you a bob or two.'

I was too disgusted by what I considered to be his bad manners to feel like recounting the story of how I had come by the gun. It was, in fact, very valuable and I was still slightly ashamed of the bargain which had been almost forced on me. I jumped at the excuse provided by Henry's arrival with two more of my dummy traps and turned away to unlock the door which led to my workshop.

Dougal returned his attention to Hannah.

Daffy and Isobel got away after lunch. We received the usual phone call to confirm their safe arrival and that Ash had travelled well and taken his dinner.

And after that, nothing. On the next day, Daffy would invariably have phoned to report on success or failure and the probable time of their return, but we waited through Saturday afternoon and into the evening.

Henry, who had been left behind to attend to one or two of his own business affairs, had spent some of the day helping us with the chores. He was becoming openly anxious, the deep lines of ageing in his face filled with darker shadows. 'Somebody would have let us know if there'd been an accident, surely,' he said.

'Of course they would,' I said stoutly. But it was only too easy to visualize the car wrecked, the dog dead or loose on the motorway and Isobel and Daffy injured and not wanting to worry us until we could be given definitive news. Pessimism feeds on ignorance. The effort of trying to think of something else only emphasized our worrying.

Henry ate with us and we spent a miserable evening together. Even Sam was fretful and rebellious but went to bed at last. Just before midnight, two hours or more after we would have expected them back, we heard the sound of a car in the drive.

Hannah was first outside into the cold night but I was close on her heels, flicking on the outside lights as I passed the switch. The car was ours. It looked travel-stained but undamaged. As far as I could see, there was nothing wrong with Ash. Daffy got out of the car, stiff from the long drive and looking fed up but all in one piece. Isobel followed. She looked sorry for herself but there were no bandages.

Beth spoke first. 'What's wrong? Why didn't you phone?'

'Didn't want to worry you.' I wondered how much

worry is caused by the wish not to cause worry. 'And too difficult to explain on the phone. We'll tell you inside,' Daffy said, shivering. She was wearing a quilted anorak, so I put her coldness down to nerves.

We moved towards the house. Hannah fetched Ash out of the car. 'Have you eaten?' Beth asked, putting first things first.

'We had a snack at a Little Chef,' Isobel said. 'Nothing filling. I could handle a bowl of soup.'

'And Ash?' Hannah asked quickly.

'Of course he's had his dinner,' Daffy said indignantly. 'We wouldn't forget that.'

Instead of taking Ash back to his kennel as the house rules dictated, Hannah brought him into the kitchen with us. She put on the kettle. 'But what *happened?*' she demanded, adding, 'Soup coming up. Who'd like a bacon sandwich?'

Between relief and the cold, it seemed that hunger was as powerful as curiosity. We all wanted bacon sandwiches. While Beth and Hannah bustled about and the rest of us took seats at the big table, Henry demanded again to be told what disasters had befallen.

There was something more important on my mind. 'Did we win?' I asked.

'It's all part and parcel,' Isobel said thickly.

I looked at Daffy.

'Did we hell!' Daffy said. 'Mrs Kitts was great and Ash worked his little backside off. Late on, he put up a hen pheasant that the other dog had gone past and then retrieved it from water. I could see that the judges were pleased. At that point I was sure it was in the bag but – would you believe? – we were pushed into second place by Mr Cove with Mim.'

There were gasps round the table. 'Never!' I said.

'It's true,' Isobel said, nodding. 'And well deserved.'

'I'm afraid it was,' Daffy confirmed. 'She was perfection. And not a trace of being gun-shy. I couldn't take my eyes off her.' She looked at me reproachfully. There could be no doubt that I had fallen from my pedestal. 'And then, to cap it all, I got breathalysed.'

'Did you pass? But you must have been all right or they wouldn't have let you drive home,' Beth said.

'I was slightly over on the breathalyser,' Daffy said, 'so I insisted on a blood test. That's where the time went. But my blood was all right. It's been quite a day.'

'You were lucky,' Beth said severely. 'I thought you knew better than to drink when you're driving Isobel around.'

Daffy managed to look indignant, puzzled and innocent, all at the same time. 'But I didn't,' she protested. 'That's what's so maddening. I thought I'd only had two soft drinks. Somebody must have spiked them.'

'Well, I just don't understand it,' I said. 'I don't mean the drinks. You probably picked up one that was meant for somebody else. But Mim's only about nine months old. And even if Quentin Cove has a cure for gun-shyness – which I don't believe – he couldn't possibly have done it in the time.'

'You're quite right,' Daffy said, 'except that she was there and handling beautifully, hunting like a dream, and one of the guns took a rabbit with a shot just over her head – a damned sight closer than was safe, if you ask me – and she never even blinked. If only I'd known . . .' She heaved a sigh that nearly blew the plates off the table.

'It doesn't follow that you'd have been able to work the same miracle,' Henry said gently. 'Quentin Cove has years more experience than you do and now that the business is running itself he has the time to apply that experience patiently. I take it that she was responding normally to the whistle?'

'Perfectly,' Daffy said. 'He hadn't plugged up her ears with wax, if that's what you're thinking. After the awards were given out I went over to say hello to both of them, but Mr Cove popped Mim into that Shogun of his before I got there. He said that he didn't want her to remember other times. He thought that we might remind her of her fear of guns. I didn't want to stand around in a bitter wind and argue about it so I just congratulated him and came away.

'Then, when we got away, we called at the first hotel we came to.'

'My fault,' Isobel said. 'I felt the need of a little comfort.'

We all nodded. Isobel always needed a drink in the let-down after a competition. She was still breathing a faint aroma of brandy into the smell of frying bacon.

'I was thirsty too,' Daffy said. 'Anyway, Mr Cove came in, almost on our heels. He was very nice and quite apologetic. He said that he felt he'd been rude when we spoke earlier and he insisted on buying us both drinks. I left mine on the bar while I went to the Ladies, so you could be right,' she told me. 'The place was crowded. Perhaps someone mistook it for somebody else's and spiked it, or else I swapped glasses by mistake. I was feeling all right, but Mrs Kitts had got over her disappointment—'

'Second place wasn't bad for Ash's first time out,' Isobel explained.

'It was very good,' Hannah said stoutly, distributing mugs of soup, 'but it doesn't count for anything.'

'—and she was being very jolly,' Daffy resumed, 'so I only thought that that was why I was having a fit of the giggles. I certainly didn't think there was anything wrong with me. And I honestly don't think there was anything wrong with my driving either, but a few miles up the road we were pulled over and they made me blow into a little machine. You know the rest.'

I still felt the need to justify myself. 'If I had to advise you again,' I said, 'I'd still say that Mim was incurable. It's all very well being wise in hindsight—'

'It's all right,' Daffy said kindly. 'I'm not blaming you. I'm sure you thought you were right at the time.'

Beth spluttered with laughter. I was less amused. But the bacon sandwiches were served out just then and the company lost interest in my honour as a prophet, instead demanding every least detail of each flush and retrieve, which dog had run in, which had been put out for pegging game and who had wiped whose eye. I comforted myself with the thought that the first time Mim trod on a thorn just as a shot went off she would undoubtedly revert to her earlier state.

Chapter Three

Most of my picking-up engagements were for Satur-
days, the prime shooting day of the week but the one
day when we were most likely to be short-handed
because of field trial commitments. For midweek
shoots, enough keepers were usually free to pick up
for each other and they usually preferred to keep the
modest extra income within their own ranks. The
keeper at Lincraigs, however, was not popular and
always had difficulty raising a full squad of beaters, let
alone skilled dog-handlers; but I was prepared to put
up with abuse and mind-changing in order to get in
the maximum of retrieving practice for as many dogs
as possible.

On the Wednesday following Daffy's brush with
the law, I set off to Marksmuir with six dogs in the car
– two aspiring champions, three that I was bringing
on to sell as workers and one that I was training for
another owner. The weather was fine and it was a
perfect occasion for training the dogs, but beyond that
point it was an event that I would cheerfully have
missed. The Marksmuir shoots were sometimes for
invited guests – distinguished company who could

foster Sir Ian's ambitions. This one, however, was primarily a commercial shoot intended to subsidize the other kind, although I was surprised to note the presence of 'Sanctimonious' Pratt in the group and guessed that he was an invitee to make up numbers. Timothy Pratt, who had managed so much to aggravate Rex without uttering a word, in common with his friend Sir Ian Bewlay was a parsimonious man, not given to spend money on frivolous pleasures unless status or useful friendships would follow on. Dougal Webb, I thought, was out of the same mould.

I have a dislike of commercial shoots, for which the visiting Guns pay so much per bird and have no interest in the land beyond its scenic value. Even so, most keepers take a pride in presenting the birds high and fast and then adjusting their difficulty so that the bag ends at or very close to the planned total at the end of a full day. But McNair, Sir Ian Bewlay's keeper, placed the Guns and drove his birds so that if the Guns had been even moderately good shots they would have reached their target before lunch and then been forced to choose between an early finish or an extra cost. The presence of Timothy Pratt, who was a competent shot, could be explained. He was there to ensure that the guests shot, and so paid for, their intended bag.

There were only two other pickers-up – one of Sir Ian's estate workers with a clumsy but efficient golden retriever and Joe Little, a fellow breeder and trainer who was similarly glad of the opportunity to train his dogs under real conditions. I was pleased at this paucity, because there would be more work for my dogs, but not impressed. The modest fee paid to a picker-up is amply recovered from the cost to the Guns of a single bird in the bag which might otherwise have been missed.

Joe was a distinguished trainer and a regular field trial judge. He bred Labradors, not spaniels, so we were not rivals and could afford to be good friends. At the break for lunch, usually taken by the Guns in what seemed once to have been the servants' hall of the big house and by the keeper, beaters and pickers-up in a former wash-house, I made sure that the dogs were warm and dry and then headed to overtake Joe.

The house was a rambling structure of local stone, its pleasing lines half hidden by ivy and Virginia creeper. Its condition was slightly rundown and the garden was definitely overgrown, further evidence of Sir Ian's genius for the false economy. The place deserved a better owner.

As I crossed the cobbled yard, Sir Ian, who seemed to have been lying in wait, popped out of the back door. He was usually around on shooting days, keeping watch to see that everything was paid and accounted for.

'Cunningham,' he said.

I slowed to a halt, reluctantly. From a rough count of beaters' heads I had already worked out that my chances of claiming one of the more comfortable chairs had gone and I was now more concerned whether there would be as much as a sausage roll left for me. The exercise and fresh air had sharpened my fallible appetite.

As already mentioned, Sir Ian was not one of my favourite people. He was large – not that I counted his height against him but his girth was unattractive. He was also red-faced, pop-eyed and with an exaggerated idea of his own importance. But he was a valuable source of dog-work, so I returned his greeting politely.

'You were shooting on Lincraigs the other day.' He paused. 'Well?'

'I was,' I said.

'You shot a pheasant on my land. Do you know how much each bird costs?' Sir Ian was a self-made man who had been knighted for some unspecified services to industry. His accent was intended to convey an impression of old money and an ancient baronetcy but it did not quite manage it. He had picked up the Marksmuir estate at a bargain price many years earlier and if a visitor jumped to the conclusion that Sir Ian, and possibly his ancestors, had been born and raised there, the misapprehension was never corrected.

My aggravation at being spoken to as if I was an errant schoolboy was increased by the arrival a moment earlier of another man, Timothy Pratt. (Pratt and Sir Ian were often to be found together. Each had political ambitions, but whereas Pratt was only aiming, for the moment, at a seat on a nearby Regional Council Sir Ian had his sights set on Parliament. Each could help the other with his ambitions. Sir Ian could give Sanctimonious Pratt many useful introductions while Pratt could ensure that Sir Ian's least good deed, be it a minuscule donation to charity or a kiss reluctantly bestowed on an even more reluctant baby, was faithfully recorded and found its way to the media. Pratt was a small man, younger than Sir Ian and about my own age, burdened with a thin face and very close-set eyes. He was very much inclined to sermonize any captive audience, and especially the readers of his column in a local paper, on any subject which he could claim as dear to his heart, though by a strange coincidence each could be expected to appeal to a wide public and alienate only a minority. Among these was the eternally thorny subject of Animal Rights. Timothy Pratt was, of course, thoroughly in favour of them without ever specifying just what rights an animal should have. But he was conspicuously against live exports, fox hunting and battery poultry-farming. He was a pillar of every animal protection society in Scotland. Yet there was one right of animals which seemed to disturb him deeply. He was eternally advocating legislation to penalize anyone daring to allow a dog to foul any public place. He had once taken to court a critic who suggested that, if Timothy Pratt could have his way, any owner of a dog so offending would be made to eat the offence. His endless preaching on these and kindred subjects had earned him the sobriquet of 'Sanctimonious' Pratt. He saw no contradiction between his fondness for shooting and his support of Animal Rights, and on that one subject I agreed with him.)

In point of fact, I probably had a better idea of the cost of rearing birds than Sir Ian did. It was generally believed that his keeper was ripping him off. But I kept a firm grip on my temper. 'I did not shoot a pheasant on your land,' I told Sir Ian firmly and patiently, 'and I do have a good idea what every bird costs. One of my dogs put up a pheasant on Lincraigs. It hit the overhead wires – still on the Lincraigs side of the march, as you know – and broke a wing.' While I spoke, I was thinking that only one house stood high enough for the occurrence to have been seen from it. 'I dare say that it would have looked like a shot bird at the distance, to someone at Gifford House. If he was behind double glazing he wouldn't have heard the sound of a shot anyway. The bird landed on your side of the fence. I did not cross the boundary, with or without a gun. I picked up the dog and lifted him over the fence.'

'Ha! You admit it!'

'I heard him,' said Pratt excitedly. 'I can bear witness.' I noticed that his wrists still bore the scars of his old burns and reminded myself to make allowances. At least he had courage.

'Why shouldn't I admit it?' I asked reasonably. 'What I did was quite legal and normal practice. Would you rather that I'd left the bird to feed the foxes?'

Sir Ian drew himself up to his considerable height, thereby thrusting his belly at me. 'There are no foxes on my land!'

That was a black lie. The prints had been clear in the snow, of foxes coming out of Marksmuir land and stalking rabbits on Lincraigs. What is more, he knew that it was a lie. So there was nothing to be gained by arguing about it. Sir Ian had made no comment on my reference to Gifford House, any more than I had mentioned that the bird's wing-tag had shown it to have been released on Marksmuir.

'I think you'll find that I was behaving properly,' I said. 'I have a witness to exactly what happened. But if you really want the bird, it's hanging in my garage. I'll make you a present of it. I should warn you that it's a cock with spurs an inch long. I wouldn't expect it to be good for more than game soup or pâté. Shall I bring it to you or will you collect it?'

It seemed to dawn on him for the first time that if he insisted on taking possession of the pheasant the story would do the rounds, growing all the while. Sir Ian was known to be a wealthy man. He might have parliamentary ambitions but his growing reputation for petty meanness was making him locally into a laughing-stock. He glanced at his watch to suggest a more important appointment elsewhere. The watch, I noticed, was a Rolex and not the one that I had seen on his wrist the previous year. 'Keep the damn bird,' he said, turning away.

'You should have taken the bird,' I heard Pratt say. 'You're too soft with these people and it only encourages them to take greater liberties next time.' Thankfully I was out of earshot before I heard enough to make me really blow my top.

I was in time to capture a sandwich and one sausage roll. I took them back to the car where I could sit comfortably in the tail, talk to the dogs as I ate and enjoy the winter sun while I waited for my temper to cool. Joe joined me after a few minutes, which was a help. We relaxed in the partial shelter, surrounded by contented dogs. I remarked that Sir Ian was an odd sort of character. 'Penny wise and pound foolish,' I amplified. 'He worries himself sick over a tough old bird shot beyond his boundary, but he's wearing a new Rolex.' Then I remembered that Marksmuir had been burgled the year before and I added, 'But, to be fair, perhaps it was an insurance replacement.'

'I doubt it,' Joe said. 'He was away at the time of the burglary and his Rolex is never off his wrist. He put it about that he fancied treating himself to a new watch and so he sold the old one.'

'I'd place a small bet that somebody got robbed.'

The beaters were crowding into their trailer. A few minutes later the first Guns appeared, among them 'Sanctimonious' Pratt accompanied by a cowed Labrador. 'I was surprised to see him here,' I said. 'He's another skinflint. I don't believe for a moment that he coughed up the price of a driven day.'

'Not in a million years,' Joe agreed. 'He and Sir Ian formed a mutual back-scratching association years ago. Pratt bought that dog from me. He haggled over the price and then, when he wanted me to train it, jibbed at the cost and decided to train it himself. He ballsed it up, of course—'

'Of course,' I said.

'—and he came back to me, wanting me to cure the dog of running-in. But once again we fell out over the cost.'

'He came to me after that,' I told Joe. 'He said that you were a bare-faced robber with delusions of grandeur. When I quoted my rates he said that I was worse than you were.'

'That figures,' Joe said. 'He was probably right. The upshot was that he was saddled with a chronic runner-in. You weren't here when it came to a head – I think you were abroad. I saw the whole thing and so did some of the beaters. A rabbit came past the guns. Pratt fired at it and missed and his dog took off after it.'

'Oh dear!' I said. I could see what was coming.

'Yes indeed. I've known men try to cure running-in with a cartridge loaded with rock salt. It stings like hell but does no permanent damage. I've also known idiots who let the dog get about seventy yards out, to where the pellets have lost much of their energy, and then let the dog have a dose of Number Six. But either Pratt has a poor judgement of distance or else he was in a rage. He shot the dog up the arse from thirty yards. He was sorry afterwards – or so he said, and it was probably true because it cost him money. The dog was in even worse agony, of course.'

'It's a wonder he didn't kill it.'

'I believe it was touch and go. As it was, the dog had to be castrated. And it's still a chronic runner-in,' Joe added.

The rest of the Guns emerged and we prepared to follow them to the next drive.

I was home, and with the dogs fed and kennelled, in time for the drinks in the sitting room with which we usually mark the end of the working day. Henry and

Isobel were away so that it was a more intimate gathering than usual. It was a time for relaxing in front of a flickering fire, toasting the toes and sipping a drink, but it was also the time for discussion. When I had reported on the performance of each of the dogs I went on to recount my exchange with Sir Ian Bewlay.

Daffy confirmed that my version of the event was the true one. Beth was justly indignant. 'That man is getting himself despised,' she said, 'and not least by me. With the game dealer paying about one-fifty a brace – for *good* birds, not ones that have been strutting around since the Gulf War – he was off his rocker to make a song and dance about it. Why alienate yet another voter?'

'He wasn't exactly thumping his chest,' I said mildly, 'and if I had gone onto his ground to shoot he'd have been within his rights to create hell. A bird costs enough to rear, never mind how little the dealer pays for it after it's shot. What really annoyed me was that "Sanctimonious" Pratt was egging him on. I noticed that Bewlay didn't deny that somebody at Gifford House had been telling tales.'

'That could only be Mrs Macevoy,' Daffy said. 'I met her at a party given by some newcomers who didn't know about her. She has an awful reputation. A plump and middle-aged, dyed redhead whose hair looks as if it's been set in fibreglass. She hardly ever goes out locally – nobody can stand her. I suppose that she and Sir Ian might be drawn together because they've both more or less run out of other friends. She goes on a cruise for about a month each winter and I suppose she gets all her socializing over in one burst, in the company of people who can't escape without jumping overboard.'

'You said that she had an awful reputation. What does she have such an awful reputation *for*?' Hannah asked.

'The usual things plus plus,' Daffy said. By some process beyond my comprehension, Daffy seems to know the history and personal foibles of anyone you care to mention. 'There was a big scandal at one time, but it was before you came here. I wasn't really old enough to be told about it but I sneaked looks at the newspapers when my parents weren't looking and I had friends who seemed to know everything.

'Her husband got himself into real trouble. They were both promiscuous, but he was worse than she was. Even so, it seems to have been a real shock when he was accused of rape. It happened a long way from here, but from the word that went round it wasn't very much of a rape – the lady's reputation wasn't any better than his and people were saying that she'd only brought the case because his cheque bounced or he refused to take his weight on his elbows or something.' Now that she was a married woman, Daffy felt free to make that sort of remark but I could see Hannah blushing.

'Then,' Daffy continued, 'there was another scandal. It came out that somebody had been embezzling from the firm he worked for – he was financial manager in a solicitor's office – but they never found any trace of the money and that prosecution was dropped for lack of evidence.

'The next thing was that when the rape case came on, Mrs Macevoy gave evidence against her husband. I thought,' she said, 'that a wife couldn't do that.'

'A wife can't be compelled to give evidence against her husband,' I explained, 'but there's nothing to stop her doing so if she wants to.'

'Can I really?' Beth said delightedly. 'You'd better behave, or you'll be amazed to hear what you've done.'

'Now I understand,' said Daffy. 'Somebody told me that he'd have got off but for her evidence. Anyway, she really dropped him in it – swore that she heard the other woman weeping and begging for mercy and so on and so forth. She made it sound like a Victorian melodrama. He got sent down for about ten years.

'At first, everybody seemed sorry for her and impressed by her devotion to the truth. But then it came out that she'd sold her story to at least one of the tabloids. "My Life With A Sex Fiend", that sort of thing. It was only discussed in hushed tones, but when I was considered old enough to hear about such things my mother explained that the Macevoys seemed to have been running out of money – scraping the bottom of the barrel, was how she put it – and that there was no doubt that her evidence had been heavily weighted against her husband so that she could get her hands on the money she got for telling, or inventing, the story.'

'If they were going broke,' Beth said, 'it doesn't sound as though he was embezzling.'

'One of them could have been gambling,' I pointed out. 'Or he may have been hiding his ill-gotten gains from her so as to be able to get out of her clutches.'

'I wouldn't have blamed him for that,' Daffy said. 'Anyway, allowing for good behaviour he should be out soon and then the fur will fly. They say that she stands looking out of the front window in case he's coming. Ready to bolt out of the back door, I suppose. That would explain how she came to see us on Lincraigs. And talking of coming, I must be going. Rex is due home any minute. It's all right, Ducky,' she said to Hannah. 'I won't see you stuck. I'll come and relieve you so that you can go out to play with your Dougal.'

'Saturday?' Hannah said quickly.

'I don't know about Saturday,' Daffy said, shrugging into her coat. 'I think we're going away. But now and again. Cheerio!'

That weekend, for the first time that season, Isobel was due to compete in an open stake – that is to say, a trial for dogs which have qualified by winning a novice stake.

By long-standing custom Daffy, who pulled more than her weight at other times, was allowed to work part-time while Rex, her husband, was ashore. The pair were to meet friends for a weekend in Paris.

We were quite used to our logistics being thrown into disarray by the unexpected. After some discussion, it was arranged that Hannah would drive Isobel on the understanding that she would accept no drinks from anybody but Isobel herself and keep her hand over the glass containing any that either of them bought for her. Henry by then felt the weight of years too heavy for undertaking long drives. I think that he would have liked to go along with Hannah and his wife as a passenger, spectator and relief driver, but he nobly stayed behind and spent much of the Saturday in helping with the still necessary chores. By early that evening the work was done and we had even managed to give every trainee a few minutes' workout. Henry, who was to stay and eat with us, fell into an exhausted sleep in the sitting room. Sam, who had been carrying feeding dishes and holding leashes with the rest, had flaked out in the other chair, the two of them snoring in occasional synchronization.

I could see that Beth was tired but when I tried to help her with the meal she shook her head. 'You look pooped,' she said. 'Go and have a zizz with the other two.'

'I don't feel like it,' I said. 'I slept last night. If I sleep now, I'll lie awake tonight. And have you heard the noise they're making?'

'Then go down to the pub.' This was Beth's panacea whenever I seemed to be in low spirits. It was her contention that draught Guinness and a change of company helped to restore me in body and spirit. After consideration I decided that for once I felt like following her advice.

'I think I will.'

'Wrap up warmly.'

I blew a raspberry. There is nothing more

annoying than being told to do something that one was going to do anyway except, perhaps, being warned not to do something which one would not have done on a bet.

The pub in our village was a former coaching inn, long since bypassed, which had been extended several times and then, happily, left alone. The stone-flagged bar wandered round unexpected corners where several open fires competed for the available draught. I penetrated to the furthest corner where I knew that the fire threw out the greatest warmth and knocked on a serving-hatch. It was early and there were only two or three customers making pit stops. During the week it would have been busy with customers on the way home – perhaps, I thought, gathering strength to face the pandemonium of family life after the peace and quiet of the office.

I sat down, made a small inroad into my pint of Guinness and let my mind drift. Business, I decided, was going as well as could be expected in an economic recession and a highly competitive, leisure-oriented market. (It was a renewable source of surprise and relief to me to find that that, however much Mr Average had to tighten his belt, there were always plenty of customers with money to spend on luxury goods.) My family life was better than most. I should have been quietly contented. But there was a ripple in the pattern. Something not quite right was cruising at the back of my mind.

My reverie was interrupted before that thought could surface. Dougal Webb's thickset form penetrated my nook. 'Mr Cunningham!' he said. 'Are you ready for another of those?'

'This will last me, thanks,' I said, wondering whether the offer would have been made if I had not been nursing a nearly full pint glass. He knocked on the hatch and bought a half-pint of lager.

'Do you mind if I join you?'

I could hardly refuse without creating a hostility which might have rubbed off on Hannah. He took the chair opposite and leaned back comfortably. He was very smart in fawn slacks, a soft tweed jacket very slightly too large for him and a white shirt with cravat. I was getting the measure of Dougal Webb. He worked hard but he expected his money to do the same, a pound doing the work of a fiver. The jacket, I suspected, had come from the Nearly New shop.

'Hannah's not back yet,' I said.

'Mrs Cunningham told me. She said I'd find you here.'

I suspected that Beth had betrayed my whereabouts in order to get rid of him. We chatted for a few minutes about the weather, the harvest, the shooting season and our progress with the dogs but my mind was elsewhere and so, I thought, was his. Eventually he came to the point. 'That's a good gun you have,' he said.

I acknowledged that the Dickson was a very good gun, hiding my surprise that he recognized the quality of a design which to the uninformed eye looks no more than efficient and unobtrusive.

'How much do you want for it?' he asked me bluntly.

'It's not for sale,' I told him.

'I'll give you a hundred,' he said grandly.

His nerve almost took my breath away. I had had several offers for the gun, not one of them for less than two thousand. 'I suppose you'd want a "lucky penny" back as well,' I said. 'Nothing doing.'

His square jaw seemed to get squarer and his eyes narrowed. 'I suppose my money isn't good enough for you?'

'It's good enough,' I said. 'There just wouldn't be enough of it even if my gun was for sale, which it isn't.'

'I'll give you a receipt for whatever figure suits you. You can use it as a tax loss.'

'Watch my lips,' I told him. 'My gun is not for sale.'

'Everything is for sale,' he said with conviction. 'It just needs the right inducement. Let's keep it friendly. You'd best accept my offer.'

Either he was out of his mind or I was being black-mailed. 'Or what?' I asked curiously.

'Or you'll be very sorry. I know what's been going on.'

'Then you'd better tell me, because I can't think of anything.'

He looked at me, hard faced, through slitted eyes, and then glanced round to make sure that we were not overheard. 'No, I can't swallow that. You know damn well what I'm talking about. And you wouldn't like it if I told the Kennel Club. That would cost you a damn sight more than the price of a gun, you and my boss both.' He got to his feet. 'You think it over and I'll ask you again. You'll be glad to take me up on my offer. You'll thank me one of these days.' He turned away.

'I'll see you in hell first,' I said to his receding back.

My peaceful interlude of contemplation was over. I finished my pint and walked out into the patchy lighting of the car park. There was no sign of Dougal Webb nor of his highly unsuitable car. I walked to the end of the pavement and took to the grass verge by the light of my torch, pondering as I walked.

At home, Henry and Sam were awake. 'Hannah phoned,' Beth said. 'They'll be a little late – you know what a slow driver she is – so we'll eat and I'll keep theirs in the oven.'

'How did they get on?'

'Certificate of Merit.'

I grunted. A Certificate of Merit might be valuable if we wanted to sell the dog but it was no help towards the Field Trial Champion status that alone would enhance every subsequent pedigree.

Sam was a terror for remembering odd snatches of conversation and repeating them just when and where they would be least appreciated so I asked Henry, who was ready to walk home, to wait until the boy was asleep and I persuaded Beth to put Sam to bed in good time. That gave me a few minutes before Hannah, with Isobel in tow, arrived home and I told them, in as much detail as I could remember, of my conversation with Dougal Webb.

'It's off-putting,' I finished, 'to be blackmailed and not know what it's about. We haven't done anything we wouldn't want the Kennel Club to know about, have we?'

'You've cursed them up hill and down dale for a bunch of short-sighted idiots, ruining good breeds with unrealistic breed standards and a closed gene-pool policy,' Beth pointed out.

'That's different,' I said. 'I don't mind them knowing about that. I want them to know what asses they are. I hate to think that they're going around with delusions of competence.'

'Well, just don't expect them to thank you. I can't think of anything else,' Beth said.

'What are you going to do about it?' Henry asked. 'If anything.'

'I can't complain to the police if I don't even know what the threat would have been,' I said. 'And he didn't want to say it aloud. Anyway, I've no witness. He's certainly not getting my Dickson. That's the one thing I'm sure of. I'm not so sure what to do about Hannah.'

'Yes,' Beth said thoughtfully. 'She wouldn't believe you anyway.'

'And,' Henry said, 'what attitude do you adopt if he visits here socially? If you exclude him from the house you'll have to give Hannah a reason.'

'And lose a good kennel-maid,' Beth said. 'Say nothing for the moment.'

'A policy of masterly inactivity is often the best,' Henry agreed. 'But if they seem to be plotting matrimony, or something equally drastic—'

'Then we'll have to tell her,' Beth said. 'And only then.'

'*Is* there anything equally drastic?' I asked.

Beth threw a cushion at me.

Chapter Four

When Hannah and Isobel returned, Hannah paused only to regale us with tales of game passed over, runners missed, eye-wipes, triumphs and tragedies, how Polly – Throaks Polygonum, to give her her full name – had failed at the last hurdle and been pushed out of the places by a half-witted tyke that had fluked the final retrieve. She then ate a meal appropriate for one of her youth and appetite before heading towards the phone to call the farm cottage where her Dougal pursued his bachelor lifestyle. The pair, we soon gathered, had then made another date for the following evening.

'I hope you apologized for standing him up,' Beth said severely. The two kennel-maids had started with us while they were in their teens and Beth, though very few years older, still felt the need to hand out motherly guidance on behaviour. On the whole they usually took it very well, with only the occasional sigh and casting up of eyes.

'I don't know why he came here at all,' Hannah said. 'I told him I couldn't be back in time. He must have forgotten. He tried to tell me that I never said any such thing, but I remember my very words and what he answered.'

Hannah spent the Sunday emulating a quick-change artist. She began the morning in jeans and a thick sweater. When the first round of chores was done, she put on a demure suit and, being in the midst of a mildly religious phase, went off to the kirk. But Daffy was in Paris and dogs, more particularly puppies, take no cognizance of the Lord's Day, so Hannah spent the afternoon back in her jeans and wellingtons, walking a succession of dogs in small groups in the cold and drizzle around the nearby fields while I undertook a little elementary training in the old barn. We carried out the evening feed and clean-up together. Hannah ate with us and then, much too early, went for a bath and reappeared in a much less demure frock and some jewellery borrowed from Beth. Even Sam seemed impressed.

When Sam was asleep, Beth and I retired to watch the television in the sitting room. Hannah came with us, but spent her time looking through the curtains at countryside prettily lit by the rising moon, holding her breath whenever the lights of a car approached from the direction of the village and releasing it explosively as the car went past. When Dougal's arrival was definitely overdue, she tried to phone the cottage and then Quentin Cove's farmhouse, but neither number answered.

At last she came and asked for the keys of my car. 'Something must be wrong,' she said.

'If you go chasing after him,' Beth said, 'you'll seem too eager. Men don't like that.'

'He'll lap it up,' I promised. 'Drive carefully. If he turns up after you've left, we'll send him back by the main road.' With a flea in his ear, I added to myself.

'You shouldn't encourage her,' Beth said as the sound of our car faded in the distance. 'Knowing what he is.'

'If I hadn't said what I did, she might have invited him in,' I pointed out.

'You have a point.'

Later, when we were watching a film on video and beginning to yawn, the telephone sounded. I had the cordless with me so I answered it. It was Hannah. 'He hasn't been here,' I told her.

'Mr Cove arrived back,' Hannah said. 'I'm phoning from his house. He doesn't know where Dougal's got to. There's no sign of him or his car and I'm worried.'

'There'll turn out to be some quite simple explanation.'

'Like some other lady-friend? That's not exactly a weight off my mind, Mr Cunningham.' For a moment Hannah sounded almost light-hearted but when she spoke again her spirits had dropped. 'I'm going to bide here for a while.'

'All right,' I said. 'Don't get cold.'

'Mr Cove says I can sit in front of his fire. Don't wait up for me. Dougal won't come looking for me this late. You go to bed. I'll see you in the morning.'

We disconnected and I relayed Hannah's words to Beth. Beth was immediately anxious but not about

Dougal. 'Should she be alone in Ardrossie farmhouse with Quentin?' she asked me. 'From what I hear, he's a danger to women.'

'But not to girls,' I said. 'Hannah can look after herself.'

'She shouldn't have to.'

'She went there of her own accord,' I pointed out. 'But if you think she needs a chaperon, phone for a taxi and go and join her. Or would you rather that I went and sat with her?'

It was a cold night and I was tired. The fire was comforting. Into my voice I deliberately put more enthusiasm than I was feeling. That was enough for Beth. 'As you said, Hannah's quite capable of looking after herself,' she said.

There were times when both Hannah and Daffy spoke to us as though we were elderly parents verging on senility, but her last words had been sensible advice and we took it. I for one was sure that, if Dougal had not found himself other company, he was playing tit for tat with Hannah for standing him up the day before. But then I remembered that Hannah had not been at fault. The date had been Dougal's error. The remainder of the video got less than my full attention.

We woke in the morning to the sound of brisk footsteps outside and the jingle of the trolley that we used to transport feed around the kennels. Beth squinted one-eyed at the clock. 'Five thirty!' she said. 'The dogs won't know what day it is!'

'They don't care what day it is,' I said. 'As long as there's food on the go, every day is Christmas.' I closed my eyes for a few seconds during which a sombre daylight arrived and Beth disappeared. There was a warm cup of tea beside the bed. I was usually the first to rise in the morning but, in deference to my sometimes uncertain health, Beth always left me to sleep in if she was the first to wake.

When I came downstairs, Beth was presiding over a pan on the stove. 'I heard you in the bathroom,' she said in explanation, as she always did. I had come to dislike the implications of the wording. Hannah, her back to us, was in jeans again. She was washing puppy dishes at the porcelain sink which was never used for non-canine washing-up. I glanced at the newer stainless steel sink but there were no dirty dishes there. Either Hannah had done the washing-up from one breakfast, which was not part of our routine, or she had not felt like eating. I raised my eyebrows at Beth and she screwed up her face.

Hannah turned round suddenly. There were dark stains under her eyes. 'Dougal hadn't come back by the time I gave up, around four. I've phoned the police and his car hasn't been in an accident.'

'But, Hannah,' Beth said, 'haven't you been to bed at all?'

'I couldn't have slept.'

'You haven't eaten either.'

'Honestly, I'm not hungry.'

Beth shared out the scrambled eggs and toast between three. 'There's no point making yourself ill,' she said firmly. 'Sit down and eat this and then go to bed.'

Obediently, Hannah sat. 'I'll phone again soon. Mr Cove is probably up by now. Daffy should be back soon. I'll go and rest when she comes in.' She looked at her plate suspiciously and then fell to with the hunger of youth, wiping her eyes, secretly as she thought, with a paper napkin.

'Mrs Kitts will be here any minute,' Beth said, 'and probably Henry too. You've already done most of the work. We can manage for the moment. But I don't know what we'll do in the longer term if you fret yourself into a breakdown.'

Hannah looked mollified. When she had eaten and made her fruitless phone calls, she went obediently to her bed.

All through the Monday and Tuesday we endured Hannah's misery. To be fair, she did her work and tried not to inflict her worry on the rest of us, but she was so obviously unhappy and frightened, and made so many wasted phone calls in the hope of getting some news, that her anxiety seemed to colour everything that we did. We tried to be careful of what we said, but so many topics had suddenly become taboo that inevitably we put our several feet right in it from time to time. Only Sam found the right words. With a child's uncanny ability to put a finger right on the hub of a problem, he marched up to Hannah while she was sitting still beside the phone after another useless call, a dispirited figure like Patience on the toilet, and climbed onto her knee. 'I'm still here,' he said. Hannah choked, clutched him tightly, broke down and howled. Sam hugged her. He knew the therapeutic value of a good cry.

'She'll be better now,' Beth said. Privately, I doubted it; but we were both right. Hannah had not yet come to terms with worry but had partially suppressed it. She was subdued but if she shed any more tears she did so in privacy.

The weather had turned suitably miserable to match Hannah's mood. Each day came grey and dank. A recurrent drizzle kept the ground sodden so that even if the weather went into remission for an hour or two a spaniel was soon made soaking wet. As I had once said – and the girls repeated it back to me whenever that particular work was getting on top of them – God made spaniels and sponges on the same day. A platoon of wet and muddy dogs to be cleaned, dried and brushed was more than the ladies of the business cared to cope with, so only those dogs for whom outdoor training was essential were allowed out for more than token exercise. The others underwent training in the barn.

On Wednesday, Detective Inspector Ewell arrived.

Ewell had been our local sergeant some years previously. His removal to headquarters in Kirkcaldy, transfer to CID and eventual promotion just when it seemed that he was destined to coast towards retirement as a perpetual sergeant, had all been due, he had told me in an expansive moment, largely to a case with which we had given him a little help and all the credit. He was a thin man, his hair now fully grey, and he was in plain clothes, looking just as neat as he invariably had in uniform. He had a friendly face which always looked as though a smile was imminent though it never actually appeared.

I had never presumed on our acquaintance. Gratitude can too easily turn to resentment. For the moment, however, it seemed that we were still on good terms although there was a touch of embarrassment in his manner. I sat the three young dogs and took a seat on one of the straw bales furnishing the corner of the barn. The Inspector considered the effect of straw on his smart cavalry twills and decided to remain standing.

'Would you rather we went into the house?' I asked him.

'This is fine. I wanted a word in private with you. Can you think what about?' He had an unusually soft voice for a policeman although he could bark when a bark was called for.

'You're not bringing bad news?' (He shook his head.) 'Then I can only suppose that somebody has reported Dougal Webb as a missing person. Have they?'

This time he nodded sadly. 'His employer once and Miss Hannah Hopewell four times. The young lady sounded very upset.'

'She's usually a sensible girl, but she was becoming very much attached to young Webb. She's naturally concerned.'

'That I can understand,' Ewell said. 'I'll be as gentle

as I can. I thought that I might have a word with you first and then perhaps you'd be present—'

We were interrupted by the arrival of Hannah herself in the barn doorway. Her face was white and her eyes looked enormous.

'No news,' I said quickly. 'Hannah, would you kennel these three for me, please? Give us a few minutes and then come back. The leads are hanging on the door.'

When she was out of earshot I said, 'I can't tell you much more than that Hannah was away with Mrs Kitts on Saturday and missed a date with Webb, or so he seemed to think. She phoned him and then told us that they'd made a fresh date for Sunday evening. She got all dolled up for the date but he never showed. Around nine thirty she borrowed my car and went to see if he was asleep or collapsed or drunk or injured or a combination of two, three or all four. Elevenish, she phoned from Mr Cove's farmhouse, to say that there was no sign of him and she was going to wait a little longer.' I hesitated, uncertain if and how to introduce the subject of blackmail. 'That's about all that I can tell you from my own knowledge.'

He looked up from the book in which he was making a few terse notes and regarded me shrewdly. 'Is that really so?' he enquired. 'Perhaps you'd care to tell me about the quarrel you had with him on the Saturday evening?'

I tried not to let my irritation show. Gossip travels like a heather fire in the neighbourhood. Webb and I had been well away from the bar but the hatch had been nearby and Mrs Hebden was a notorious chatterbox. Instead of volunteering my information I would apparently now be making an admission under questioning.

'There's not a lot to tell,' I said. 'Young Webb had admired my shotgun—'

'The Dickson?' His tone was respectful. As a sergeant, Ewell had been responsible for implementing shotgun and firearms legislation in the area and he knew about guns.

'Yes,' I said. 'He joined me in the bar. He said that when he called for Hannah and found her missing Beth had told him that I'd be there. Hannah is sure she'd made it quite clear that she couldn't get back in reasonable time, but that may be by the way.'

'She's a reliable sort of girl? Not given to fantasizing?'

'Yes, very reliable,' I said, 'and no, no more than any other young lady of an age for romantic dreams. Webb brought up the subject of my gun. He offered me a hundred for it.'

The Inspector clicked his tongue. 'The young man was looking for a thief's bargain?'

'Very much so. When I told him that he didn't have a hope in hell, he began to utter vague threats. He seemed to be suggesting that I'd been doing something that the Kennel Club wouldn't approve.'

'And had you?'

'Nothing that they don't know about. I've criticized their policies up hill and down dale. Young Webb seemed to be suggesting that his boss was concerned with me in something nefarious, though apart from buying dog-food off him I've had no dealings with Cove in years. I suppose we raised our voices. That was as far as it went. If it hadn't been that we weren't even talking the same language, I suppose that it could have been called a blackmail attempt. But we'd come up against a barrier of total mutual incomprehension.'

'It didn't occur to you to tell the police?'

'Tell them what?' I demanded irritably. 'There was no witness. At least, not that I knew of at the time,' I amended. 'And the words themselves could almost have been innocuous. After all, it's no crime to make somebody an unacceptable offer for some possession and I could hardly point to any threats when I didn't know what if anything was being threatened. But one thing occurred to me since. If he's in the habit of using threats to gain what you called a "thief's bargain", it might be worth finding out how much he paid for his watch or for the fancy car he drives around in. And any other expensive acquisitions.'

Detective Inspector Ewell thought it over while contemplating me mildly. I remembered him as an officer who was never brusque but instead was given to comfortable chats over a cup of tea or a beer, which probably gained him far more information than any amount of interrogation would have done. 'You realize what you're suggesting?' he asked finally.

'I'm not suggesting anything,' I retorted, perhaps untruthfully. 'I'm giving you the facts. If you want to suggest—' I was about to put words into the Inspector's mouth as he nearly had into mine. The thought hanging in the air between us was that blackmailers have been known to disappear, sometimes for ever, when a victim has been pushed too far. I was interrupted by the return of Hannah. She paused in the doorway looking, I thought, rather like a trapped moth awaiting the arrival of the spider.

'Come in, come in,' Ewell said at his most fatherly. Perhaps the thought about the spider had not been wholly inappropriate. 'Do sit down.' (Hannah perched one neat buttock on another straw bale and looked at me pleadingly.) Ewell introduced himself. 'I've asked Mr Cunningham to bide with us while we talk. Is that all right? I thought you might prefer it.'

Hannah nodded more confidently.

'Aye well,' the Inspector said. He pretended to flip back through his notes but he was watching Hannah out of the corner of his eye. 'How long have you been going out with Mr Webb?'

'About a year,' Hannah said very softly. It was little more than a whisper.

'When did you last see him?'

'About ten days ago. On the Saturday. There was a dance at the Royal Hotel.'

'And you made a date for a week later, Saturday last?'

'But I phoned him during the week,' Hannah insisted. 'I was driving Mrs Kitts to a field trial and I knew that I couldn't possibly get back at a reasonable time. The trials usually go on until almost dusk, then there's the results and presentations. And Mrs Kitts likes to stop on the way home. So I told him that I'd phone and make another date.'

'Then why did he come here asking for you?'

'Perhaps he forgot that I'd phoned him,' Hannah said after a pause. 'Perhaps habit took over. Saturday nights were – are – usually our time together.'

'Would you say that he was absent-minded?'

'No. But anybody can forget things if they have something else on their mind.'

'What did Mr Webb have on his mind?'

The day was still overcast and daylight was failing early. Under the harsh fluorescent lights in the barn, Hannah was looking older than her years. 'Nothing that I know of,' she said carefully. 'But I hadn't seen him for a week. You'd better ask Mr Cove.'

Ewell nodded. 'But when you phoned again – on the Saturday evening, was it? – what was his reaction? Did he sound like a man who had forgotten your call and was angry at having been stood up? Or was he apologetic for having made a silly mistake? Angry with himself, perhaps?'

'None of those.' Hannah was becoming more confident. 'He sounded quite normal. I said that it was me and I was back now but it was too late to go out, just as I'd expected. And he said yes it was and that he thought he'd have an early night for a change and how about tomorrow evening? I said that that would be fine and I asked him why he'd come looking for me. He said that he'd come over on spec and he asked how we'd got on and I told him and he said he'd spent most of the day dismantling a tractor and he'd rather have gone along with us. He said that he'd pick me up at about eight the next evening. And that was it, really.'

'That was absolutely all? You're sure of that?'

Hannah turned pink and became tongue-tied.

'Have a heart, Inspector,' I said. 'I'm sure you wouldn't expect a young couple to hang up straight away. You wouldn't have done so yourself when you were courting. Equally, you can't expect one participant to quote the fond exchanges out of context. Words which were memorable gems between the two would sound quite insane when quoted in public.'

Hannah looked at me gratefully.

'I suppose that's so,' Ewell said. 'Well then, Miss Hopewell, I'll put it another way. Was the rest of your conversation limited to an exchange of . . . endearments?'

The pink of Hannah's cheeks became tinged with scarlet but she nodded.

'And during that exchange, was his manner as usual?'

Hannah got up, walked to the doorway and turned. I thought that she was holding back the tears with an effort and wanted to be able to duck out of sight if the effort failed. 'Absolutely as usual,' she said defiantly. 'I told him that I loved him and he said that he loved me.'

'But on the Sunday evening, he never arrived?'

'No. I tried to phone but I got no answer. So I borrowed Mr Cunningham's car and drove there. Dougal's cottage was dark and there was no sign of his

car. I sat there for hours, until about eleven, playing
the radio and sometimes running the engine to keep
warm. Then Mr Cove drove home. He let me come in
and use his phone to call back here and say that I'd
be late. He sat with me for a while and had a drink of
whisky, because he said that he'd been needing a good
dram all evening but he couldn't take more than a
drop because he'd be driving. He went off to bed after
that but he said that I could wait in his house if I
promised to drop the lock behind me as I left. So I did
that. In the end, between three and four, I decided that
it was too late. If he came home at that time, I wouldn't
want to face him. So I gave up and came back here.'

'Was it unusual, for him to stand you up like that?'

'He's always very dependable,' Hannah said. 'He
wouldn't do it on purpose, I'm sure of that.'

'The two of you are close?'

'Yes, we are.' Hannah's cheeks, which had lost their
colour, flushed again and her mouth hardened. 'But to
save you asking, Inspector, we haven't slept together.
In fact, I'm a virgin. I don't think that he is, but I
certainly am.'

It was the Detective Inspector's turn to redden. 'I
was not, in fact, going to ask you such a question.
Does he see other girls?'

'I don't know, Inspector. If he does, he never told
me and I wouldn't expect him to.' And with that Par-
thian shot and a quick sob, Hannah turned and stalked
off towards the house, injured dignity in every step.

'A young woman of spirit,' Ewell remarked. 'But I

seem to remember that, not so long ago, she was a real hellion.'

'Teenage rebellion,' I said. 'As soon as she started working with animals she cooled right down. It's the best therapy in the world.'

'I must try it some time.' The Detective Inspector paused for thought. 'Might she have heated up again if she was the woman scorned? If, say, while she was waiting in your car he had arrived home with another woman's lipstick on his face and her perfume hanging around him? What do you think?'

I tried to imagine Hannah as the woman scorned and found that it was easy. She was more a natural victim than an aggressor. 'She would be hurt more than angry,' I said. 'There might have been words. There would certainly have been tears. No more than that. You've checked that he isn't lying in hospital somewhere, unidentified?'

'Not unless he had changed his sex and aged about thirty years.'

'Oh,' I said. It seemed to be the only possible comment. But I was not ready to give up yet. 'Tell me, have you found his car?'

'Aye, we have. I see no reason not to tell you. It was in the station yard at Cupar, undamaged.'

'There you are, then. He's got fed up and run off. People do.'

'They do that,' the Inspector acknowledged. 'And I ken it better than you do. But when somebody vanishes, we must aye consider the possibility that . . . he didn't just run off. If he did run off, was he threatened?

Bribed? Was he running away from guilt of some crime? We have to consider these things.'

'I suppose you must,' I admitted. 'But you needn't consider that possibility in respect of Hannah Hopewell or me. I didn't have a car, remember. And even if he did make Hannah angry enough to dot him one, what would she have done with the body? I can't see her managing to handle the agricultural machinery well enough to bury him about the farm and leave no trace.'

'No more can I,' Ewell said. 'But mind this, Mr Cunningham, she was sitting almost on the doorstep of a deserted pet-food factory.'

The next few days were spent in a sort of limbo. We were the rabbit waiting for the eagle's strike, the condemned waiting under the guillotine. Something was going to happen. We had no way of guessing what it would be, but it would not be pleasant for Hannah. Dougal Webb might come back with an explanation, credible or otherwise, to account for his disappearance. He might be found wandering with amnesia. Or he might turn up dead or injured, in which eventuality Hannah and I might have more questions to answer. Detective Inspector Ewell had hinted – and my mind shied away from the hypothesis – that a pet-food factory might be the ideal place for the disposal of an unfaithful lover or an aspiring blackmailer.

Hannah, to do her justice, tried to cope with her job but for once her heart was elsewhere. She sank

into a state of unhappy apprehension, comforted only
by a lopsided faith in a God of her own imagining.
The big dining table in the kitchen was often the scene
for lively discussions or arguments on any subject that
took our fancy and we had been made aware of
Hannah's views. She made no secret of them. She
admitted that, logically, she could not give credence
to the idea of a personal God. She was an avid reader
in such spare time as we left her and she was aware
of a growing view that, if the evidence of the Dead
Sea Scrolls was to be accepted, the traditional view of
Christ was the imagining of Saul of Tarsus after he had
suffered a stroke on the road to Damascus and that
Jesus, rather than the son of the deity, had more probably been a political agitator. These things she knew
and part of her mind accepted. But, she would argue,
the churches were the only force striving for all the
old moralities and might be forgiven for clouding
the issues with myths. And yet that very mythology
gave rise to the philosophy and ritual of the Christian
religion which had such appeal and comfort for her
that she made a conscious leap clean over disbelief
and into a faith that was not blind but deliberately
unseeing.

Daffy, while her husband was at home, should
have been working part-time, but with Hannah distracted by worry and liable to vanish without warning
in the direction of the church, she gave up much of
her leisure to help out rather than have me put pressure on Hannah to pull her weight. In particular, she

and Rex agreed to escort Isobel to an open stake to be held near Perth at the weekend.

Our order of various grades of dog-food was delivered that week by Quentin Cove – to Hannah's distress, because it was yet another reminder of her Dougal's absence, although she helped with the fetching and carrying. When the last bag was stowed in the store Quentin, at Beth's invitation, took a seat in the kitchen. I joined them for coffee while the girls went back to work.

'Taking it badly, is she?' Quentin said. 'I'm sore vexed for the lassie.' I noticed the slip back towards the language of his childhood on the farm and took it for a sign that his concern was genuine.

'She'll get over it,' I said. 'The not knowing is the worst. Are you getting by without him?'

Quentin helped himself to more sugar and cream. 'Aye,' he said. 'We're managing. It's a quiet time of year. But, truth to tell, I'm glad to get back to running the farm. It only takes four men to keep the factory working and I've moved them around to cover for me. If it works out we'll maybe leave it that way. That's if young Dougal doesn't come back,' he added quickly.

'Do you think he will?' Beth asked him.

'I've no way to tell. I saw him go off in yon wee car on Sunday morning. I thought he was maybe heading to see Hannah or some other lass – you know what these lads are – but he was wearing jeans and his working boots. He came back later to change his clothes.' Quentin Cove paused and looked thoughtful. 'Leastwise I heard his car – there was no mistaking the sound of it. I never needed to watch his comings and goings – he's a worker, I'll say that for him, so that I could always trust him to take time off to go beating or do his courting or whatever and I'd know that he'd make it up when it suited him. Did you ken that his cottage was broken into?'

'The things people do!' Beth said. 'Do you suppose it was somebody who'd heard that Dougal was missing?'

'That I don't know. I doubt it. On Monday, when he didn't show up for work, I took the spare key that I'd kept and went across to see had he maybe slept in or fallen ill. From outdoors it looked all right and tight, but the inside was all . . . all tapsalteerie and when I looked around I could see that a window had been forced. There was no sign of Dougal. That's when I decided to report him missing. I'll tell you this, between these four walls.' Quentin lowered his voice. 'I'm not wishing any ill on him, but I can do without his kind around the place. There!' Looking rather pleased with himself, Quentin bit into one of Daffy's rock cakes.

'We know what you mean. If she wasn't so heart-sore I'd say that' – Beth paused and chose her words – 'the best thing for Hannah would be not to see him again.'

Quentin nodded and changed the subject. 'It didn't put you out, not being able to train on my land?' he asked me. 'I've seen you on Lincraigs.'

I said that we were getting by. But Ardrossie had been a valuable standby when rabbits were in short supply around home and I wondered whether another arrangement would be possible. 'Who did you let the rough shooting to?' I asked.

To my surprise, Quentin showed a trace of embarrassment. 'You'd not know him,' he said. 'A lad from Anstruther. Maybe I can make it up to you. They're nearly finished felling on Gifford Hill. That's where most of the rabbits have been coming from. One of my factory staff has ferrets, but many of the rabbits are lying out and some of the buries have more holes than you'd believe. I want them cleared out and the factory could make use of the meat. How do you fancy shooting over ferrets on Saturday?'

'Very much,' I told him. Several of the dogs could still do with steadying to rabbits, while those dogs being trained as workers rather than field triallers would be the better for experience of working around ferrets. It was sometimes an extra selling point.

'I'll have him phone you.'

'I didn't know that Gifford Hill was yours,' I said.

'It belongs to Marksmuir. It's been let to Ardrossie since my granddad's time, but it's not good land and on a north slope so I leased it for the forestry. If I'd known that I was leasing it as a nursery for the bloody rabbits,' Quentin said, 'begging your pardon, Mrs Cunningham, I'd have let them keep their money and gone on growing neips for cattle on it. Which is what my father aye did.'

Later that day, when I was helping with the preparation of the main meal, I took up a handful of the small cubes. Then it came to me that what I was holding in my hand might contain a trace of Dougal Webb's mortal remains and I dropped them hastily. But dogs must be fed and I had had no great fondness for young Dougal. I let the evening feed go ahead. No such thought had occurred to Hannah but I noticed that Daffy only took up the cubes with the scoop provided for the purpose.

Chapter Five

Henry elected to come with me to Gifford Hill. On the Saturday, he lent a hand with an early session of feeding and walking. As soon as we were sure that Beth (helped by Sam), with Hannah and Isobel, could easily cope, we loaded four dogs and both guns into my car and set off, right on time. It had rained in the night but had turned into the sort of day that makes comfortable dressing problematic – warm in the sunlight but with a cold breeze when the wandering clouds hid the sun, and with a threat of showers. It would be cold up on the hill but warm work climbing it.

Forestry work on Gifford Hill was finished. The ground was now bare except for the few outcrops of rock which had previously only been visible as gaps in the conifers. Even the stumps had been pulled and heaped on the huge bonfire that was now reduced to dross and ashes and charred lumps of root, but smoke or steam still drifted into the cold air. Gifford House, home to Mrs Macevoy of dubious reputation, stood boldly out of the landscape, its walled garden an oasis in the desert.

Jack Gilchrist, Quentin Cove's employee and ferreter, was waiting beside a motorbike and sidecar in the road below. He had only been a voice on the phone to me, but the moment I saw him I remembered encountering him more than once when he had been acting as a beater on various shoots, usually in the company of Dougal Webb. He was a cheerful, tubby little man. With his big ears and prominent teeth he looked rather like a rabbit himself, so that I half expected his ferrets to take him by the neck; but they were well-kept little animals, very affectionate but very much under his thumb. He had already worked the small, isolated burrows and a dozen paunched rabbits were cooling behind one of the few surviving sections of hedge to prove it.

A common error would have been to hunt the spaniels first, pushing any lying-out rabbits underground ready to be bolted again by the ferrets. But Jack had found, as I had over the years, that unless you can spare the time to wait for anything up to a couple of hours before putting in the ferrets, the rabbits may prefer to face the ferrets underground rather than the danger above. Even the sound of shots would be less of a deterrent. If a ferret killed underground we might have been faced with a lengthy lie-up. We decided to walk quietly up to the largest outcrop, which was also the highest, and work our way down. That way, the bag would only be carried downhill. We would then finish with a hunt in the open.

The hillside had originally been planted ridge-and-furrow and then had been further disturbed by the rooting out of the trees, so that the ground had been left in a wildly uneven state. Rather than make frequent trips to the bottom and back up over the difficult going, I put leads on all four dogs and took them along. Each caught the scent of many rabbits and became eager to start the hunt, but they were there to learn restraint.

The rocky outcrops had been fragmented by age and weather. The rabbits had entries or exits through long fissures as well as between and below fallen boulders. Jack's purse-nets could never have attempted coverage. At each outcrop, I found a secure place for the screw-in anchorage and attached the dogs. The ferrets went in and I had time to glance at the spectacular view over the sparse chessboard of winter countryside. When the rabbits began to spurt out, Henry and I attended to their slaughter. For all his advancing years, Henry was still an excellent shot. Then I would free one dog and do the picking-up and out would come our knives for paunching.

The operation began well. The dogs soon realized that this was not an occasion for riotous behaviour and performed rather better than adequately. The ferrets came back to hand with very few lie-ups. Although at that time of year the rabbit population would have been at its lowest, our game-bags were getting heavy.

It was too good to last. We were just finishing at the third of the rocky outcrops, which happened to be nearest to the house, when a stout female figure emerged through a side-gate in the garden wall and hobbled towards us in unsuitable shoes, picking her way as best she could over the bumps and hollows. From Daffy's description of her hair, which was red and so lacquered as to look synthetic, I could guess her identity.

Mrs Macevoy was in a state of high indignation. We were disturbing the tranquillity for the sake of which she lived so far from civilization. What was worse, we were doing it at the weekend and close to her house. We were upsetting her cats. She was going to call the police. When I had managed to convince her that our activities were perfectly legal, she switched ground. We were being cruel.

That was too much for Henry. 'Madam,' he said, 'the rabbits would not live for ever and they do not die in their beds. Which of the methods open to them do you think they would prefer? Myxomatosis? Starvation? Freezing to death? Or being taken by a fox or one of your cats?' Mrs Macevoy emitted a squawk of protest but Henry rolled on. 'Do you realize, madam, that more wildlife is killed by domestic cats than by the entire field sports fraternity, and more painfully? So who, then, is being cruel?'

For some reason that defies analysis, when Henry speaks people listen. Mrs Macevoy listened with her mouth open. Whether she was convinced, whether she even took in Henry's argument, I had no way of knowing, but I thought that she was going to turn on her unsuitable heel and totter back to her house.

Jenny (short for Gentian) had been helping with the pick-up, but while I was distracted she had started to hunt. She was always a fast mover. (Beth called her

Twinkletoes.) She was also a friendly little dog. When in ebullient mood and if she felt that she was getting less than her fair share of attention, she would pluck at one's trouser-leg as she went by, as if to say, *Look at me – aren't I beautiful?*

Jenny chose that moment to appear from nowhere and to give a tug at Mrs Macevoy's skirt as she passed by. It was no more than a friendly gesture, but the woman chose to let out a screech. 'Your dog attacked me!' she announced. 'Look!' She exhibited a very small hole near the hem. It looked to me like an old cigar-ette-burn – Mrs Macevoy's fingers were stained yellow – and I was sure that Jenny, who had never left behind a visible tooth-mark, had only touched the other side of the garment.

'Rubbish!' I said.

She rounded on Henry and Jack. 'You saw?'

They shook their heads. Jack was grinning.

Her face flamed. 'Get out of here, you *bloody* men. I'm going to call the police.'

I am not proud of what came next. I can only say that Mrs Macevoy had exhibited all the traits that I most despise, in particular uttering the word *men* as though it was a dire insult. I can only put up with stupidity allied to bad manners for just so long. 'How much attention do you think the police will pay to a woman who shopped her own husband in order to sell the story to the gutter press?' I asked politely. Evilly inspired, I added, 'Isn't he due out soon?'

She turned white and then back to red. Without

another word, she turned and made off back towards the house, stamping her way so that she almost fell.

'Not a nice woman,' Henry said without lowering his voice. He shot a sly glance at me. 'But perhaps she feels that she is politically correct.'

Henry knew that the words *politically correct* are to me as a red rag to a bull. In any other context a reference to politics implies a whole field of deviousness and expediency. There would have been no need to devise such a phrase as political correctness except as a more acceptable way of saying *I know it's rubbish but I want it to be true so you must believe it anyway.* Outdated attitudes were changing without the extra leverage, and the label of *political correctness* was now too often being used to damn attitudes which had been adopted because the experience of a thousand generations had shown that they were what the majority wanted, rightly or wrongly, to believe. But this was not the time for a dialectic argument. Some day soon, I would take my verbal revenge. 'Shall we get on?' I suggested coldly.

'In due course,' Henry said, grinning. 'We seem to have another visitor.'

I followed his eyes. The tiny but indomitable figure of Mrs Dundee was struggling up the uneven slope. I greeted her arrival warmly and introduced her to Henry – partly to give her time to recover her breath, but I had genuinely liked the old thing.

'Would you like another rabbit?' I asked her. She looked relieved and I guessed that that had been the object of her climb. 'Take a brace,' I said. 'In fact, two brace.'

'You hae plenty?'

'Far more than we need,' Jack said.

I noticed that her cheery smile had vanished, leaving only the goblin looks. Had she been so haggard when we met not long before? I thought not. She was holding a plastic carrier-bag which gaped open, exposing several handfuls of kale and a turnip which had been partially nibbled by sheep. She saw my glance at it and bit her lip. 'I lost my morning job,' she whispered. 'My afternoon work doesna pay. And I'm no old enough for the pension just yet. My Jimmy will see to't when he gets hame soon frae the sea. Meantime, I maun just get by.'

'You don't have to explain,' I said. 'But have you been to the Benefit Office? Nobody's left to starve, these days.'

'I'll no tak charity.' The occasional rabbit between friends, it seemed, was neither here nor there. 'My Jimmy left me some money when he was last ashore, but he didna hae muckle and it's a gone.'

'Please take this to tide you over.' I found that I only had a fiver on me so I handed that to her. Henry matched it. She thanked us gravely and turned away, back down the hill.

'I didn't know,' Jack said simply. 'But I'll see she's never short of a few rabbits till her boy gets back.'

I brought Jenny back under command and we finished gathering the slain. When these were paunched and the guts disposed of down a rabbit hole,

Henry's game-bag and mine would have been more than filled. We were about halfway back to the car but none of us fancied repeating the stiff climb if it could be avoided.

'Hang on a moment,' Jack said. 'We need a pole.'

Henry and I gladly took seats on the stones and rested our wearying legs. Getting about on that sort of surface was as tiring as twenty times the distance on level ground. Jack was quite right. A heavy load of rabbits is most easily carried slung on a pole between two men. The foresters had done their work well and there was very little in the way of loppings left lying, but Jack was heading for the area where the bonfire had been. I watched him idly and saw him single out a long branch from the partly burnt fringe, produce a large knife and begin to trim off the twigs. Then he stopped and stared. He turned, sheathed his knife and hurried back towards us.

He arrived breathless and shaking. 'There's a dead man,' he said, gasping. 'Leastwise, I think there is. It's that brunt you can hardly tell.'

Although the unexplained disappearance of Dougal Webb had kept the possibility of a dead body in our minds for several days, now that the possibility had become a probability our first reaction was disbelief. Henry and I wanted to see for ourselves.

We left the guns and our heavy game-bags with the ferret-box and I sat the dogs to guard them. 'Probably some farmer's way of disposing of a dead sheep,' Henry said as we hopped and staggered across the uneven ground.

'I hope so,' said Jack shakily, 'but I don't think it.'

The bonfire had been built on a relatively flat area, from all the otherwise wasted limbs and roots and loppings. The heat met us twenty yards off. From among the smells of warm earth and conifer logs I scented others and I judged that it had been fired by the most usual method – paraffin and a few old tyres. There was also another smell, familiar but so out of place that it was like a blow to the face. The centre of the fire was now a hump of white ash and charred roots and around the edges was a ring of unburned twigs and branches. Part-way in from one edge was the body.

It was certainly dead. I could understand Jack's uncertainty. The body was curled and partly con-sumed, almost indistinguishable from the scorched and shapeless roots, but it had once been human. I had seen burnt bodies during the Falklands War and I was in no doubt of it.

Henry was in agreement. 'No point standing here gawking,' he said. 'We'd better call the police.'

Jack looked unhappily in the direction of Gifford House. 'I'll not go knocking on that woman's door and asking to use her phone,' he said firmly, 'and that's definite.'

'No need.' Henry patted his pockets until he found what he wanted. 'Thought so,' he said. 'I have my mobile with me. There should be a passable signal up here. Nine-nine-nine, you think?'

'It's hardly an emergency,' I said. 'He's not going

anywhere. But it's the only number I can remember offhand. Should we be getting back to the dogs?'

Henry had already keyed in the number. He made a brief report to the police before answering me. 'We're warmer here,' he said.

Jack was more practical. 'They rabbits should be hung up or laid out to cool,' he suggested. He looked at Henry. 'You can bide in the warmth if you like.'

But Henry came with us. He admitted to me later that his eyes had been constantly drawn to the gruesome sight among the ashes and he had no wish to be left alone with it. We decided that the police would prefer us to disturb the whole scene as little as possible, so instead of carrying the rabbits down to the car we laid them out to cool and then found ourselves the best seats we could among the bumps and hollows.

'You reckon that's him?' Jack asked suddenly. 'Young Dougal?'

'It looked too small for him,' Henry said.

'They always do,' I said. 'Fat burns. They lose a lot of bulk in a fire and they curl up.' Jack looked ready to be sick, so I hurried to find at least a partial change of subject. 'It would be a bit of a coincidence, a man going missing and a different body turning up in strange circumstances. But coincidences do happen.'

'I think you understated the case,' Henry remarked. 'What we have here is a man going missing and a murdered body turning up. And that is a little too much coincidence for anyone to swallow. Unless, of course, you can find a more innocent explanation for how it came to be where it is. You're not going to suggest that a tramp crawled in there for shelter and was still asleep when they lit the bonfire?'

'He could have passed out with hypothermia,' I suggested doubtfully. 'Or drink.'

'Suicide,' Jack said firmly. "That'll be it. He could ha crawled in and takken poison, thinking to be wholly brunt.' Like many others, when disturbed he was becoming broader in his speech. "They go to all kinds of lengths, whiles, to leave no trachle ahint. Or maybe it was for the insurance.'

I guessed that Jack was suggesting that there might have been an insurance policy with a suicide clause. But if the deceased had intended to do a favour for his nearest and dearest by concealing the fact of suicide he, or possibly she, would certainly have got it wrong if the body had indeed been wholly consumed. Insurance companies do not readily pay out on mysterious disappearances unless or until a court gives the family leave to presume death. Without mentioning blackmail I said as much and suggested, as being marginally more possible, such scenarios as somebody having had a heart attack in the wrong bed or else a hit-and-run accident, conceivably to Dougal Webb himself. In either case it might have seemed more convenient for the corpse to disappear for ever. This triggered a meandering argument which touched on various other explanations, of escalating improbability, and lasted until the first police car arrived on the road below us, disgorging no less than five officers.

That was the moment for all hell to break loose. Handling a number of leashes while carrying a gun

and a game-bag comes close to my idea of hell. As
each dog had done its working stint, blowing off steam
and becoming more biddable, I had left it off the lead.
While we sat and talked I had been vaguely conscious
of a huddle of dogs around me without bothering to
count them. I had not noticed Joshua, who had been
brought to me for retraining, sneak away to begin an
exploration of all the alluring scents around. At that
critical moment he nosed a rabbit which had been
sitting tight in the concealment of a drift of twigs,
cones and coniferous needles. The rabbit did the sensible thing and bolted for the nearest holes, a course
which took it close past our feet.

The result was inevitable. I had taken those dogs
out just because they needed steadying to fur; but
even a fully steadied spaniel may sometimes succumb
to the temptation of a rabbit being hotly pursued by a
rival. Joshua swept up the other three into a yelping
pack which in turn bolted several more rabbits.

Any reader who thinks of the springer spaniel as
a slow and lumbering dog has only seen an over-
weight, show-bred fireside pet. Instead, he should
witness a fit young springer of working stock going
flat out. It may not be a match for a greyhound but it
can give a rabbit a good run for its money.

They knew that they had broken discipline. Guilt
was written all over them. As each dog raced with ears
flying, above its head there might well have been a
little 'thinks' balloon, reading, *I'm wicked but it's
worth it*.

I was not altogether unsympathetic. To have four

legs and hunt a rabbit must rank among the world's most exhilarating sports. But to me as a trainer, this was disaster. Weeks of work were being undone in seconds. In theory I should have run after each dog in turn, catching it in full cry and administering a good shaking. The trouble was that, even if I had not been as stiff as a very old man from sitting uncomfortably in the cold wind, they could still have run much faster than I could. On the other hand, punishing a dog after it has returned to you conveys precisely the wrong message.

It was a time for compromise and for leaving the mess to be sorted out later. I tried to run and blow the stop whistle at the same time, never an easy combination. The first dog to pass close by expressed its sentiments in every frantic movement – *Can't stop now, busy, busy, busy!* At the third try Jenny heeded the whistle and I managed to grab her and blow the whistle in her ear as a powerful reminder. Jack, who realized the seriousness of the situation, took her back to Henry on a lead while I went after the next. To the police it must have looked like a textbook example of what should never happen. To the sound of whistles, shrill yelps and much shouting, their death scene was being swept and trampled by dogs, rabbits and human feet. To make matters worse, Henry had collapsed into helpless laughter. 'View hulloa!' he shouted and 'Tally-ho!' The last, stemming as it does from the French *Il est hault* (he is lame), probably applied more to me than to either the dogs or the rabbits.

The arrival of Detective Inspector Ewell in a

shining but otherwise undistinguished Range Rover probably saved us from arrest or worse. Ewell knew at least something about gun dogs – indeed, during his time as our local sergeant he had occasionally whiled away part of a boring shift by helping me on the Moss, tirelessly throwing dummies or discharging the dummy launcher, and he recognized the disastrous nature, from my point of view, of the riot. As he hurried up the hill, a rabbit went to ground a few yards ahead of him. One of the dogs buried its head and shoulder in the hole so that its excited yelps came from all the neighbouring holes. Ewell pulled the culprit out and held her up by the scruff of the neck until Jack could collect her. At the same moment, my grab for another neck latched onto a tail. The last miscreant, realizing that the fun was over and that all odium was now focused on him, came to heel, trying to look hurt and surprised that I should think that he had been among the rioters. *Who? Me? I was trying to catch those others for you* . . .

We came together, puffing, and Henry, now serious again, took charge of the four leads.

'Now that that's sorted,' Ewell said, 'you can tell me what's adae. Somebody reported a dead body, partly burned, so I came to see for mysel.' He looked from one to the other of us, awaiting explanations.

'I found it,' Jack Gilchrist told him proudly.

'And I phoned you,' Henry added.

'And it's over there,' I said, pointing. 'We haven't touched it and I don't think we've seen anything helpful or caused any more disturbance than we could help, but we'll stick around anyway.'

'Aye. That you will,' said Ewell.

'I take it,' said Henry, 'that sport is over for the day. Is it all right if we load up our rabbits and wait in the car?'

'No, it is definitely not.' The Detective Inspector looked around him and decided not to make three usually responsible citizens stand around in the cold, for which I was thankful. During the chase, I had sweated under my waxed cotton coat and the chill breeze was beginning to bite. 'You can wait in my Range Rover,' Ewell said. 'Take your guns and the dogs but leave the rabbits where they are.' He nodded to a uniformed sergeant who had followed him up the hill.

'Well, all right,' Jack said. He glanced sideways at Ewell. 'But, mind, the rabbits are counted.'

The sergeant preceded us down the hill. I hung back a few yards. 'Sometimes I feel a bit Bolshy too,' I told Jack softly. 'Inspector Ewell isn't a bad sort but he can be firm if he's crossed. Better not to annoy him or we may never get home.'

'That's a very well,' he grumbled, 'but what for will he no let us clear up and go home?'

'You don't want to know,' I said. Jack was obviously puzzled but Henry looked at me and nodded. I could see for myself what Inspector Ewell would be thinking, because I would have thought the same in his shoes. Dougal Webb was missing. Now there was word of a dead body. If the body had not died on the spot, it would have had to be conveyed there. He knew that each of us had some connection with Dougal Webb. To cap it all, the finders of a body are usually suspect. Ewell would undoubtedly want our vehicles to be examined before he allowed us near them again.

We put the dogs into the rear of the Range Rover alongside a nest of traffic cones and then sat three abreast in the back seat. Jack nursed the ferret-box on his knees. Henry and I held our bagged guns. Jenny stood up against the back of the seat and panted in my ear.

The Sergeant was far from the conventional image of a police sergeant. She was a young woman, very smart and tidy in uniform. It was unusual, in my limited experience, for a sergeant who was driving and dogsbodying for a plain-clothes inspector to wear uniform. I decided that this departure must be to lend her the authority that her apparent youth would other-wise have denied her. Like Beth and other slim, long-legged ladies she looked very young – too young to be in the police at all, let alone have earned her sergeant's stripes. On closer scrutiny of her hands and eyes and throat I decided that she was more mature than first impressions suggested but no less attractive. Even in uniform, her figure was temptation incarnate, her legs creations of beauty. Her dark eyes and full lips raised an otherwise modestly pretty face from the ordinary. Her skin was very good. In short, she was a walking mantrap and I suspected that she knew it, but her manner was perfectly neutral.

She took the front passenger seat, turning round towards us and, I supposed, tucking her legs under her in that loose-hipped way that women have. She rested a notebook on the back of the driver's seat and began a series of questions. It was soon clear that she was well educated and no novice. Her questions were precise and to the point and she took down our answers in a neat shorthand.

When she was satisfied she had the bones of the story and that we were not withholding any startling revelations, she came back to the visit of Mrs Macevoy.

'What did you think was behind her approach to you?' The Sergeant looked at each of us in turn.

'Behind it?' Jack said.

'Was she really disturbed by the sound of shots. Did she really have a fellow-feeling for the rabbits?'

Jack shrugged. The Sergeant switched her gaze to Henry. Henry sucked his stomach in. If he had had a moustache, he would have given it a twirl. 'I was surprised by that attitude,' he said. 'The woman – I won't call her a lady – has been living there for some years. From what I've seen, her garden is not in the class that gets opened to the public, but from a distance it looks cared for and there's been some attempt to grow flowers and vegetables. It's walled, but the gates are by no means rabbit-proof. There would be food there for rabbits and none in the forestry plantation. Overnight, they probably gorge themselves at her expense. I think that by now she must be totally fed up at the damage that rabbits do. In similar circumstances, most householders are begging for somebody, anybody, to come and reduce the numbers.'

The Sergeant turned her big brown eyes from

Henry to me. I tried not to smirk. 'Did she just want to make you go away?' she asked.

'It could have been that,' I said. 'At the time, I put her down as one of those people who have no importance of their own and who try to give themselves a little brief and synthetic importance by handing out a lot of aggravation. You know what I mean?'

'I know *exactly* what you mean,' the Sergeant said, nodding in spite of herself. 'But, from what you remember of her manner at the time, what do you think now?' When none of us hurried to answer she spoke again, slowly and clearly as if to children. 'Could she have been trying to head you away from finding the body?'

I had disliked Mrs Macevoy intensely, but that was all the more reason to try to be fair to her. 'Now,' I said, 'I'm not sure. She could. I can't say that she gave that impression.'

'But she used the words, "Get out of here you bloody men"?'

'Yes,' we said together. 'Accent on bloody,' Henry added.

'And said that she was going to call the police?'

'Yes.'

'But she didn't.' The Sergeant was making a statement. She made a long note. 'What about Mrs Dundee?'

'All she was after was rabbits,' Jack said. 'I think,' he added.

The Sergeant's shorthand might be neat but it was

not very speedy. This had all taken time, during which I had watched the comings and goings. It was soon evident that Ewell, as was to be expected, was treating the death as suspicious. I had recognized the police surgeon. A photographer arrived and then another car with men who I assumed to be Scene of Crime Officers.

The Sergeant looked at me again. 'Your car key?'

I handed it over. Detective Inspector Ewell had descended to meet the newcomers. The Sergeant got out to join the throng. I saw her read from her notes. Ewell nodded. At a word from him, two of the newcomers went and fussed around my car.

I rapped on the window. The Sergeant came back and resumed her seat. 'Yes?'

'To save them a lot a wasted excitement,' I said, 'you may as well explain to them that I'm in the habit of carrying shot rabbits and game in the car. Any bloodstains, in the rear end or behind the driver's seat, will be from that.'

She frowned. 'You don't stick to the one place?'

I suppressed a sigh. The most maddening aspect of a police inquiry, I had discovered in the past, was the need to verbalize explanations of the obvious. 'Some dogs travel well in travelling boxes, where they can lie down and not be rolled around. That lets me put game in beside them. But if a dog is car sick, it travels better standing up and looking out. If there's a dog loose in the back of the car I daren't leave anything edible in with it, so shot game goes on the floor behind

101

the driver. But that doesn't mean that you won't find bloodstains anywhere else.'

The Sergeant wrinkled her pretty nose. She made a final note and closed her book. 'I'm glad that I don't share a car with you,' she said austerely.

'I, on the other hand, am sorry,' I replied without taking time to think. The Sergeant dithered for a moment, uncertain how to react. 'It was a compliment,' I added. 'Just ignore it. But you might point out to Inspector Ewell that we're getting hungry.'

Without comment, the Sergeant got out again. She slammed the door of the Range Rover more vigorously than before. We were left to stare through the windscreen. Mrs Dundee was at her gate, watching.

'Even when I had my youth and vigour,' Henry said, 'I never made sexual advances to a policewoman on an empty stomach.'

'Did they not have women constables in the Bow Street Runners?' I asked him.

Soon after that, we were allowed to collect our rabbits and go. Jack offered us a share of the bag but we both declined. I never wanted to see those particular rabbits again. We told him to give our share to Mrs Dundee.

Chapter Six

When we got back to Three Oaks, Beth was pacing up and down outside the house. Her temper was conspicuously high, which for her was unusual. She was speaking, loudly so as to be heard through the glass, before the car had quite stopped. 'Where have you *been?* I have been waiting and waiting for the car and there was no sign of you except for about three words from Henry on his mobile to say that you were held up and I've got to get to the shops before they close because Sam knocked over a whole jug of milk and we're almost out. Have you had anything to eat?' she asked on a second breath as I opened the door.

'Nothing. I want a word with you.'

'Later. There's lunch for both of you in the oven, mostly, if it hasn't burnt. Hannah and Sam are walking the last batch of dogs in the field. I've got to go.'

'I have to talk with you now,' I said, getting out of the car.

'No time,' Beth said, getting in and groping for the key which I had been careful to take with me. 'What happened to the floor-mats?'

'The shops won't close for more than an hour and

I'll go and get milk before then. The police have the mats for examination. They'll be looking for blood-stains.'

That stopped her. 'What happened?'

'That's what he's trying to tell you about,' Henry explained.

As usual, Beth listened to Henry. 'What is it, then?'

'And I need Hannah,' I said. 'Help me with the dogs. They need their dinners too.'

Not even the usually overriding topic of the dogs' dinners distracted Beth this time. She was looking dazed. 'Why do you want Hannah?'

'I'll explain if I ever get a chance to talk to you calmly, with her and with Henry, indoors, fed and seated. I am not embarking on a lengthy subject standing out here, cold and hungry. And neither is Henry.'

Beth gave up fumbling for the key and got out of the car. Between us we fed, brushed and kennelled the four dogs. Henry cleaned both our guns and we managed to snatch a late and hasty lunch before the dog-walkers returned. Sam, luckily, was yawning after the dose of concentrated fresh air and was put down to rest. Beth had lit the fire in the sitting room and we others settled in front of the hearth. Hannah knew that something was coming and she was perched on the edge of her chair, her hands clasped together so tightly that I thought she would draw blood.

Without more delay I said, 'Hannah, you'd better brace yourself for a shock. We don't know anything for sure, but we found a body this morning. It had been inside a big bonfire of forestry waste so it may be some time before it's identified, but there's obviously a possibility, if not a probability, that it is or was Dougal Webb. As far as we know, he's the only person to have gone missing.'

I had been looking into the fire as I spoke. Now I glanced back at Hannah and away again. She had turned very white and closed her eyes but her chin was still high. 'Please tell me it all,' she said in little more than a whisper.

'You're sure?'

'Yes.'

So I told the story of our day, with Henry interpolating when I missed out any details.

At the end, Hannah asked, 'How can they ever make sure who it is? I mean, if it's so badly burnt . . .'

'You'd have to ask the police about that,' Henry said, 'but the necessary information usually comes from dental records.'

'They won't help very much,' said Hannah. 'Dougal always boasted – boasts – that he's got perfect teeth and never went to a dentist in his life.'

'Then if they find that the body has fillings in its teeth . . .' Beth began gently.

'That might not help. You see, Dougal isn't always very truthful about that sort of thing. He doesn't mean to tell lies.' Hannah looked earnestly at each of us in turn. 'It's just that he likes to brag a little. I can quite imagine him saying that he had perfect teeth because perfect teeth are better than teeth full of fillings and so from his point of view it was the right thing to say at the time, just to score points off the other person. Scoring points is important to him.'

That, I thought, said quite a lot about Dougal's humble origins.

'Don't worry about it,' Henry told her. 'They can do a great deal with the length of bones, the shape of a skull and any old operations or fractures. They can even rebuild the features, just from the skull. They'll find out for sure. Meantime, you can only wait and hope.'

'I expect so.' Hannah sighed shakily. She was turning palely green at Henry's ramblings.

I did not share Henry's faith in forensic science. Skulls can burst in intense heat. But, for Hannah, a detailed description of the head of the corpse in the bonfire might be the last straw. 'It's a little early in the day,' I said, 'but I think we could call it knocking-off time. Hannah, you'd like a drink? A stiff one for a change?' I had it in mind to give Hannah a good stiff mixture of port and brandy. Nothing can beat it as a settler for a queasy stomach.

Hannah shook her head and got to her feet. 'I'm going out,' she said hoarsely. 'Dogs to walk.' She hurried out of the room.

I looked at Beth, who shook her head. 'The dogs have all been walked,' she said. 'But never mind. Hannah won't want anybody to see her face for now. The light's going. Walking dogs in the fresh air and twilight may be the best therapy for her. It won't do the dogs any harm, either. What was that about a stiff drink?'

'That was for Hannah's benefit,' I told her. 'I'll have to be going if I'm to fetch milk.'

'Never mind about the milk,' Beth said – or words to that effect. 'Hannah can walk some more dogs up to the farm later. Did you mean to imply that the police think that Mrs Macevoy was trying to head you away from finding the body?'

'That would be putting it a bit strong,' Henry said. He was already at the side table and pouring our customary drinks. 'All we can tell you is that the woman sergeant who took our preliminary statements seemed to think that it was one question that Mr Ewell would ask later, so she'd better have the answer.'

Beth considered. 'It could be,' she said. 'If Mrs Macevoy had carried the body from the house and hid it in the bonfire and then found today that it wasn't completely burned – heavy rain woke me during the night, it could have damped down the remains of the bonfire – she could have been planning to go out after dark to bury it or move it, as soon as it was cool, or even to rekindle the bonfire.'

'You haven't seen the place,' Henry said. 'It had originally been planted ridge-and-furrow and then, so that the roots would be out and ready to burn, they'd taken down the trees by pulling them out with a tractor. That would be at the landowner's insistence,' he added, resuming his chair with a substantial whisky to hand. 'The ground was like the aftermath of a major battle in World War One, all trenches and shell-holes. The woman could hardly get herself over it – in fact, I found it hard going myself.'

'I certainly couldn't carry a body over it,' I said. 'Especially in the dark.'

'Would a barrow have made it easier?'

'The reverse.'

Beth was reluctant to abandon a nicely compact theory. 'With a male accomplice . . . Oh well, we can think about it when we know a little more.'

'I don't want to think about it at all,' I said.

Beth seemed to accept what I said at face value. 'You don't have to think about it if you don't want to. So what happens now? When will the rest of us know something?'

'The media will know even less than we do, for the moment,' I said. 'The police will be asking questions. The more they find out the more questions they'll ask. You know that, you've seen them in action.'

'And they'll be handing out information like a tiger giving up its kill,' said Henry.

'You can make a lot of informed guesses from the questions they ask,' Beth said. 'And sometimes even more from what they don't ask. If it's Sergeant Ewell—'

'Detective Inspector Ewell,' Henry and I corrected her in unison.

'If it's Mr Ewell,' Beth began again, 'I'll pick his brains, just you see if I don't.'

Once again we were in a state of limbo. From the media, I gathered that Jack Gilchrist, as the actual discoverer of the body, was giving interviews galore and would continue to do so for as long as the body was news and his stories continued to grow in dramatic appeal – or until an arrest was made and the whole subject became sub judice. Of hard news, there was none.

I told Hannah that she could take time off, go home, do anything that would help her to get through the period of uncertainty, but she said that she would go mad if she had nothing to occupy her mind. That was all very well and quite understandable. I would have felt the same. But there is no helper more counterproductive than one who promises to do something and then forgets. As long as Hannah was liable to fall into a trance or suddenly hurry out of sight to hide a burst of weeping, she was more of a nuisance than a help. Beth and Daffy tried to comfort her, which usually made bad worse and also hindered their own labours. As a result, we endured two days during which the work of the kennels went forward, if at all, in fits and starts. The dogs soon knew that our minds were not on them and they began playing us up.

When Detective Inspector Ewell arrived unheralded at mid-morning on the Tuesday, accompanied by his Sergeant – still glamorous though still in uniform – it was, more than anything, a relief.

Ewell wanted to speak first to Hannah and Hannah asked me to be present. When Ewell made no objection, Beth, after a speculative glance at the Sergeant, managed to suggest that perhaps another woman, and not of the police, should attend in case comfort was called for. That also was accepted after a judicious pause, but when Daffy (accompanied by Sam) and

Isobel tried to add themselves to the party, he drew the line. They were excluded, firmly but politely. Henry, who would probably have managed to include himself in the conclave by dint of the mere authority of his presence, was away.

We settled in the sitting room. The hearth had not been cleared, which was a measure of our disturbed state, but two firelighters soon kindled a fire of logs above the old ashes. The flames performed their usual magic, transforming the sometimes cheerless room into a welcoming haven. I saw the Sergeant glance up at the painting above the fireplace, of a skein of geese over an estuary.

Hannah was looking towards the Inspector as a rabbit might look at a stoat.

'Mr Cunningham told you about the find on Saturday?' Ewell asked her. The question seemed superfluous. I suspected that he had put off this particular interview until he could be quite sure that I had done the job for him. As a sergeant, I remembered, the breaking of bad news had been the only part of his work which he faced with less than enthusiasm.

Hannah nodded.

Ewell, who had seemed as apprehensive as Hannah herself, looked happier. 'I still have no definite information for you,' he admitted. 'So far, that body has not been positively identified. You'll understand that we have to consider the possibility—'

'That the body is all that's left of Dougal Webb,' Hannah said bravely. 'I understand. Mr Cunningham explained. He also told me how badly burned it was.'

The Detective Inspector looked still more relieved. 'And that's one reason I've come to you. We are in some difficulty. Mr Webb seems almost to have appeared out of nowhere. His employer knows very little about him. The job was advertised, Mr Webb applied. Mr Cove checked on his college diploma and left it at that. The addresses at which Webb was living when he took his course and when he made his application were both lodgings in Falkirk. Can you, for instance, tell us who Mr Webb's dentist is?'

Hannah repeated what she had told us, that Dougal Webb had boasted of his perfect teeth, and paused.

'Hannah had her reservations as to whether that was necessarily true,' I said.

'From what we've been able to find out so far,' Ewell said, 'he seems to have been a model of truthfulness – at least in that one respect.'

'And the body had good teeth?' Beth put in.

'Well, yes. We know which medical practice Mr Webb signed on with, but he never seems to have needed more attention than a bandaged cut or a prescription for cough mixture. They don't even have a record of his height and weight. We can make an estimate of those from the clothes left in his cottage, but that's a poor basis for an identification. The body, as you say, was badly burned and—'

I saw Beth wince. 'If that's all you want from Hannah, can she go now?' Beth asked. 'Surely she needn't hear the gory details?'

'It's all right,' Hannah said quickly. 'Somebody's

died. That's all I care about – that, and whether or not it was Dougal.'

'I would never give what you call "gory details" to a member of the public,' Ewell said with dignity. 'I was only going to say that we recovered some of Mr Webb's hairs from his hairbrush and there was a bloodied sticking-plaster in his bathroom. There should be no difficulty isolating his DNA – what they call "genetic fingerprinting". That may take about ten days. But the body's DNA may present more of a problem.'

Despite the Inspector's fine words, I was sure that he had been on the point of explaining that they had hopes of an identification by genetic fingerprint *if the body was not cooked beyond the point at which DNA could still be isolated.* And if that was not a 'gory detail', figuratively speaking, I did not know what was. Or perhaps Ewell did not count incineration as being gory but even quite the opposite.

'You won't want to lose that time,' Beth said. 'Is it true that the longer a case drags on, the less chance there is of solving it?'

'So they say, and it seems likely. I've not been in CID long enough to speak from personal experience. But that's why I'm looking to you for help, Miss Hopewell. You knew the deceased – Mr Webb, I mean – better than anyone.'

'You're sure that it's Dougal Webb, aren't you?' Beth said.

Ewell had flushed. He hurried to correct himself, speaking directly to Hannah. 'Put it down as a slip of the tongue, please. I'm thinking along those lines, of course I am, and so are you. As Mrs Cunningham pointed out, the longer a case goes on the less chance of solving it there's said to be. So we've got to make the best start we can even though we don't have a positive identification. That means that we've got to start from the likeliest assumption. But I've no way of knowing for sure yet, one way or the other. With the young man's next of kin not known . . .'

Hannah frowned. 'What? But I can tell you that,' she said.

Ewell tried to hide his surprise. 'You can?'

'I think I can,' Hannah said cautiously. 'I nearly said something when you told us about him appearing out of nowhere. I don't know if he was still being – what did you call it? – a *model of truthfulness.* He sometimes says what he doesn't really mean, just to build himself up a bit. Romanticizing, sort of. But, for what it's worth, I'll tell you. I was at Ardrossie one time, and we could see Gifford House sitting up on the hill and sticking up out of the trees. I said how I'd like to live in a house like that some day, or like this one, a house built when there was space and quality and with country round about it, not jammed in between neighbours on either side and front and back and a garden the size of a blanket. And he said something like, "Stick with me and you'll live in that house some day. My aunt lives there and neither of them has any relatives closer than me."'

'Mrs Macevoy?' Beth exclaimed.

'It would have to be, wouldn't it?'

It happened that the Sergeant was sitting in my

field of vision, at a corner table that usually only sported back numbers of magazines, and I saw her look up and frown. Beth must have caught the same look. She said, 'Mrs Macevoy didn't tell you? Surely you asked her about Saturday?'

'Of course. She didn't give you a very good press, by the way,' Ewell added in my direction. 'But Mr Webb's name wasn't mentioned and she might not have known that he was missing. She seems to live a rather isolated existence. We've been trying to trace Webb's origins. This is the first indication we've had that he was local.'

'He probably wasn't,' Beth said. 'According to Daffy, the Macevoys had only lived here a very few years before the big scandal. Dougal Webb may have moved here to be near them. He may even have heard about the job vacancy from his aunt. But, of course, after his uncle was sent to prison, he wouldn't have boasted about the connection.'

'That's true.' The Detective Inspector seemed relieved by Beth's reasoning. He returned his attention to Hannah. 'You don't know where he grew up? Or whether his parents are still alive?' Hannah shook her head. 'Never mind. One other thing. It would help if you could provide some photographs of him. As many as possible.'

'I only have one or two snapshots. I'll get them back in the end?'

'I promise.'

Hannah got up. When she was out of earshot, Beth asked, 'Are you still in charge of the case?'

114

'For practical purposes,' Ewell said slowly. I guessed that it hurt his dignity to admit that he was no longer the top dog, but in the presence of his Sergeant he would have to be truthful. 'Superintendent Aicheson is in nominal charge but he has other things on his plate.'

Beth pounced. 'So it's being treated as a case of murder?' An inspector might deal with an unexplained disappearance but murder would usually be the province of a more senior officer.

Ewell very nearly smiled. 'I would have come to that as soon as the lassie was out of the room. There was no need to creep up on it obliquely. Likely, I'll have to take a further statement from her. But take a look at this, which has just reached us.' He stretched out a hand. The Sergeant rose and handed him a large photograph. Evidently there were no concessions to gender in the Fife CID.

Ewell passed it to me. The single transparency had been made up from four X-rays. On a reduced scale it showed a slim knife-blade which had been snapped off. It was still in place among what looked like human organs. Alongside it had been drawn a scale, according to which the blade was some twenty centimetres long. 'Do you have a knife like that?' he asked.

'Probably,' I said.

'Do you still have it?'

'If we ever had one, I expect it's still around. You're welcome to look.'

He took back the photograph. 'You're very casual about a lethal weapon.'

'Potentially lethal,' I said.

'What do you mean?'

'It wasn't designed for use as a weapon.'

Ewell blinked at me. 'I've asked for a report on the knife-blade,' he said, 'but I won't get it until the post-mortem is finished and the blade can be examined. What can you suggest?'

'You called it a lethal weapon. So is a teapot, if you brain somebody with it. This wasn't made as a weapon. A stabbing knife can be one of several different shapes altogether, quite unlike this. The point is usually in line with the handle. It would be made from heavier stock, a quarter of an inch or so thick, not steel that would snap off. It can be a plain dagger shape or a clip-point "bowie" with the clip sharpened. The blade would usually be dull or darkened – blued – which I don't think is what you'll find when you do get your hands on it. And the blade would usually be tapered or grooved to let air go past. A plain, flat blade like this with parallel edges would be gripped by suction. Stab somebody with this and you might not be able to pull it out again, though you might need to use it again in a hurry.'

Beth made a little sound of protest. She had never quite come to terms with the violence of my earlier career.

'I bow to your experience of weaponry,' Ewell said slowly, 'even if I wouldn't want to have had it myself. So it's a hunting knife? Or a kitchen knife?'

'Probably not a hunting knife.' I took back the photograph. 'This has a curved sharp edge and a straight blunt edge. You do get hunting knives of that shape, but they're not easy to use. The main purpose of a hunting knife is to open up a dead animal neatly. The knife in the X-rays would slit the skin but it would dig in and perforate the guts or the meat. That may be acceptable, depending on your technique and what the meat is, but not to me. A hunting knife usually has a blade shaped like this.' I dug my lock-knife out of my pocket and opened it to show him the blade. 'A curved cutting edge. A straight back edge but angled down by about ten degrees near the point – that's the "clip" I referred to earlier. It gives a blunt edge to ride along on the meat without cutting into it. When you get it out, if the clip turns out to have been sharpened I'll take back most of what I've told you.'

From Ewell's expression, he was suffering from an excess of information and needed to boil it down. 'So this would be . . . what? A kitchen knife?'

'I suppose so,' I said. 'Or a badly designed general-purpose sheath-knife. It's longer than a stalker's knife or a combat knife, and of thinner steel.'

'For use around the farm?'

'Possibly. But my first guess would be kitchen knife,' I said.

Beth had possessed herself of the X-rays. 'It's not one of ours,' she said. 'And if he was stabbed in the back, like this—'

Ewell jumped as though he had been stung. 'How do you know he was stabbed in the back?' he demanded.

'Both my parents are doctors,' Beth said. 'X-rays are

always being passed across the breakfast table. I think that that was what turned me off following in their footsteps. But at least I know what a human heart looks like and which way round it is. I was only going to say that some force must have been used to get between the ribs.'

The Detective Inspector relaxed. 'You had me going there for a moment, Mrs Cunningham.' There were footsteps in the hall. Ewell recovered his transparency and put it away quickly.

'But you'd agree?' Beth asked.

'Oh, yes. The pathologist's opinion is that it jammed and was broken in an attempt to pull it out again.'

Hannah came back. She offered three or four small photographs to the Inspector. 'I've remembered something else,' she said. 'While I was waiting in Mr Cove's house I was sitting at the window overlooking the yard. There was a small lamp on the table beside me. At about two in the morning a car came into the yard. I think the driver saw me at the window, because he turned in a circle and drove away again.'

'You didn't see him?'

'Inspector,' Hannah said, 'I didn't even look at the car. I was waiting for Dougal. I knew from the sound of the car before it appeared that it wasn't his Lotus. It wasn't even his style of driving. So I didn't bother.'

The Detective Inspector said nothing but from the look of exasperation on his face I knew exactly what he thought of a witness who 'didn't bother to look'. Then he firmed his jaw and persevered. 'Miss

Hopewell,' he said, 'if you could tell without looking that it wasn't Mr Webb's car or style of driving, then you must have some idea what sort of car and style of driving it was.'

Hannah took a few seconds to think back, and when she spoke it was less certainly than before. 'It wasn't a sporty sort of car like the Lotus. Something heavier, but not a diesel, I think I'd have known one of those. And Dougal had to pay for his own petrol unless he was doing an errand for Mr Cove, so he used to keep his engine speed down.'

'I noticed the same thing,' I said. 'He changed up as soon as he could and delayed changing down until he had to. Not the right technique for a sports car.'

'That's what I was getting at,' Hannah said, relieved. 'But whoever was driving, that night, came up the farm road in a fairly low gear, changed further down to slow the car and then braked quite hard. Dougal tried not to use his brakes much. He always said that brake linings were expensive.'

We discussed among ourselves the mysterious corpse, the missing farm manager and every conceivable connection between the two. That was inevitable. But the subject was best avoided whenever Hannah was within earshot and when, after a day or two, it was clear that she was too distraught to pull her weight and she was packed off to have her megrims in her father's house, we were too busy and too short-handed to manage more than a snatched word or two between more pressing topics.

To make matters worse, Isobel then went down with the 'flu. For her own sake and to prevent her from spreading it to the rest of us, we declined her offer to come in and carry on with the paperwork from a cosy fireside chair. She was banished to her bed a safe couple of miles away. The very idea of the whole complement of staff and partners being bed-ridden simultaneously was not to be contemplated.

Ash had been entered for a novice stake in the Lothians that Saturday. With Isobel *hors de combat*, the sensible thing would have been to withdraw, but the season would be over all too soon and Ash needed a win if he was to go forward into open stakes and pursue what we hoped was his destiny as a Field Trial Champion with a lucrative and voluptuous career at stud to follow. A whole sackful of second places would count for nothing. Daffy did not yet have a tenth of the required experience. Handling our entrants in field trials had been my responsibility until one of my relapses had pitchforked Isobel into the job with unex-pectedly happy results. Obviously I would have to take over again.

Beth's immediate reaction verged on panic. Rex had returned offshore. She and Daffy, assisted as ever by Sam, could cope with the kennel routine. But Henry would be too fully engaged with Isobel either to help with the dogs or to come as my companion and body-guard. Beth could already visualize me having one of my blackouts among strangers who would then empty my pockets and leave me to expire, alone and unidentified. I was torn between irritation at the disruption of our plans and a warm glow that somebody loved me enough to worry about me.

The argument had reached stalemate when a phone call threw a fresh weight into the scales. Earlier in the season, a sporting journalist had been much impressed by one of our bitches and had written glowingly of her performance, using her exclusion from the top honour to illustrate his contention that judges could sometimes be struck with blindness or insanity. A businessman in Bristol was in the market for a trained spaniel and had made up his mind that only one of our breeding would suit. When I told him that a son of that bitch was trained and ready to go, he was willing to do a deal over the phone. It happened that he would be in Edinburgh on the Friday but would have to be back in Bristol by Saturday afternoon to prepare for a major meeting on the Monday. Could I bring the dog to meet him in Edinburgh on Friday? As a clincher he decided, while still on the phone, to buy a puppy as a present for his son.

Beth did not want to let me out of her protective custody, but there was serious money involved and she would have hated to pass up two good sales. Her resistance began to crumble. She phoned Joe Little, who was to judge on both days. She made him promise to keep an eye on me for as long as our programmes coincided and to call out the emergency services the moment that I failed to show up at an appointed time. And so I was ready, with a car full of three dogs, all the accompanying paraphernalia and my overnight bag, when Joe sounded his horn outside the gate early on the Friday morning. None of my fainting spells had ever occurred while I was sitting down but Beth had still insisted that we travel in convoy. We had a peaceful journey. A puppy may be forgiven for protesting shrilly when being transported away from home and siblings, but the presence of his uncle seemed to give him reassurance.

Beth had furnished me with a list of shopping which she considered to be essential for her future well-being. I left the list with one of the largest stores while I did the rounds of my favourite gunshops. After a quick lunch in a pub, I collected Beth's parcel and met my client in his hotel. He fell for the pup immediately and when I worked the other dog for him, in and out of the bushes at Hermitage Park, to indoctrinate him into the commands to which the dog had been trained, he expressed himself more than satisfied. I handed over the necessary papers and most of my cargo of dog-food, said a fond farewell to the two dogs and an even fonder hello to a very substantial cheque and drove out of the city through the falling darkness to the hotel where rooms had been booked.

That day's competition, a novice trial for retrievers, had gone well. Joe was already in the bar, buying his own drinks as was right and proper but lapping up the sycophancy of those who hoped to be remembered kindly next time around. When the crush began to melt away he joined me at a corner table.

'Still living and breathing, I see,' he said.

'If you can call it living,' I retorted. 'Beth does fuss rather.'

'Don't knock it,' he told me severely. 'She's quite right. I was with you the second or third time you flaked out, remember? Gave me the fright of my life. I had to lug you to the nearest quack.'

'Letting me lie flat for a while would have been enough,' I told him. 'According to the doc, it's much the same as a common faint.'

'Except that people don't always come round when it's vagal inhibition.'

'That's how you tell the difference. All the same, I owe you for that. What a pity I'm not supposed to buy you a drink. There's nothing to stop you buying me one,' I pointed out.

'Nice try,' he said. 'But if I bought a drink for one competitor I'd have to buy them for all the others or there'd be complaints about favouritism.'

We ordered another round of drinks and meticulously paid for our own. 'Are you ready for tomorrow?' Joe asked me.

'The dog's ready,' I said. 'I'm not sure about me. I'm out of practice and I haven't had time to get myself into the right state of mind. But I was working the dog not long ago. I think we'll get by.'

'I'm sure you will.' But Joe's mind was not really on my state of readiness. 'It's a bugger finding somewhere to train these days, isn't it? I've never known such a bad year for rabbits. Are you dependent on picking-up?'

'Mostly.'

'I met Quentin Cove in the Drookit Dug the other day,' Joe said. 'He told me that I could come onto Ardrossie. I thought that that was one of your patches.'

'It was,' I said. 'That's odd! He told me that he'd let the rough shooting and I'd have to stay away.'

'You must have put his back up somehow. You didn't leave a gate open that should have been closed, or close one that he wanted left open?'

'I hadn't been there for weeks. Last time I was there he walked round with me, taking turnabout to work one of his own dogs. He expressed himself as suitably obliged to me.'

'Then it beats me,' Joe said. 'Unless that chap Webb was the rough-shooting tenant. Did he shoot?'

'I don't know,' I said. As I spoke I remembered Webb's desire for my Dickson but I kept my mouth shut. The subject was fraught with danger.

'He certainly went beating,' Joe mused. 'Beaters usually shoot, though I suppose he could just have been beating to curry favour with Sir Ian and other landowners. But if Webb really had rented the shooting from his boss, now that Webb's dead Cove might feel free to hand out permissions again.'

It seemed to be the general assumption but all the same I pricked up my ears. 'Dead? Have you heard something I haven't?'

Joe shrugged. 'Shouldn't think so. It's just the word that's going around. You probably know more than I do.'

'Webb's certainly gone missing,' I said. 'And there's a body. But as far as I know there's no proven connection yet.'

'The police think there's a connection,' Joe said. 'They took an interminable statement from me about the last time that I saw Webb. I may have been the last person to see him alive,' he added with a certain pride. 'Other than his murderer, of course.'

'Murderer?' I said.

'Assuming that he's dead and assuming that he fetched up in the bonfire, its not easy to think up any explanation other than what they call *foul play*. I was running short of feed for a nursing bitch so I drove over to Ardrossie that Sunday evening, around seven. Webb and his boss were talking in the big yard. They broke off as I pulled up. I didn't hear what they were saying but they sounded a bit heated. Then Webb got into his Lotus and drove off with an uncharacteristic burst of wheelspin. He was usually too canny to waste tyre rubber. Damn silly car for a farmer,' Joe added. 'Or for a dog trainer. All the same, if it's coming on the market . . .'

A waiter came to tell us that our table was ready in the dining room. When the conversation found its way back to Quentin Cove, somewhere about the sweet course, it was by way of a long gossip about dogs in training. 'Quentin turned up with his bitch Mimulus at an open stake last weekend,' Joe said. 'He was hoping to get a run if somebody dropped out, but he was out of luck.'

125

'He must be getting keen,' I said with my mouth full of *crème caramel*.

'Get a good dog and neglect him, or else work him to death,' Joe said. 'That's always been the amateur's way.'

Chapter Seven

I left an early call and was the first guest to breakfast.

The previous night, I had noted near the hotel a stretch of rough ground which had been left to gorse and weeds, the sort of ground beloved by environmentalists and dog trainers. After breakfast, I settled my bill and went out to the car. Ash came eagerly out into the cold air from his cosy bed in the back of the car, relieved himself in a cloud of steam against somebody else's rear wheel and came reluctantly to heel. A spaniel, and especially one as high-spirited as Ash, must blow off steam and I was determined that any steam-blowing would be done before we came under the judges. I took him onto the waste ground and let him race around for a few minutes. When he began to show signs of wanting to hunt I brought him back under control, worked him to a pattern through the bushes and then gave him two retrieves with a canvas dummy. That, I hoped, would be enough and not too much.

At the trial ground I felt again the almost forgotten surge of excitement as the once familiar scene took shape. Competitors, openly nervous or hiding their nerves. The two judges in a solemn huddle. The Guns, happy with their role but nervous of shooting badly before so many critical eyes. Officials fussing. And the pickers-up, who would linger to look for any birds on which the competing dogs had failed, secure in the knowledge that they in their turn could fail unseen but could play a game of one-upmanship by coming back with a bird. It was 'not done' for a picker-up to display the bird from a successful retrieve, but it had been known for one of them to allow a bird from that or even from a previous retrieve to be glimpsed as though by accident. The pickers-up liked to consider themselves the only true professionals present.

The cumbersome line moved off across a field of stubble, with a tail of onlookers and competitors awaiting the call. Conditions were difficult. In the sharp air and rising breeze, some dogs were hot to handle and threw points to the wind. The sky was dark and the air very cold. I would have expected scenting to be adequate but it was very bad. And many birds seemed determined to sit tight instead of flushing. Dog after dog pegged a squatting bird and was eliminated.

First time 'up', I knew that things were going my way. Ash, having already worked off his excess energy, was nicely in hand and working a perfect pattern but he retained enough of his innate manners to disdain pegging sitting game. He flushed several birds and pulled off a good retrieve. We went through to the next round.

By mid-afternoon, Ash was among the four dogs

called for a run-off. One of the first brace, I thought, performed indifferently but each managed a flush and a retrieve. Then we were called. I reminded myself, for the umpteenth time, to stay calm and, if in doubt, *trust the dog* – always good advice but not so easy to follow in the heat of the moment.

The line was struggling through a field of turnips, thinned by winter. Despite a frosted surface over which dogs could run, the mud beneath took hold of a boot and made walking a penance. No bird with a grain of sense, I thought, would be out of the woods on such a day and looking among the roots for insects which must have died out weeks before. But Ash homed in on a small cock pheasant and kicked it into the air. The nearest Gun fumbled his shot and the bird spiralled down, a strong runner, beyond the boundary hedge and ditch.

The judge, Joe's colleague, nodded to me.

Ash had been unsighted. I pushed him, with hand signals, through the hedge and out to the fall and he picked up a scent. I wondered whether to curse or bless my luck. A difficult runner may lead to failure, or to a successful retrieve and impressed judges. I had lost sight of the bird. Ash followed his nose, plunged into the hedge and vanished. I kept my hand away from the whistle and reminded myself over and over again, *The dog knows more than you do.* When movement drew my eye to Ash again he had crossed a narrow field, hurdled another fence and was entering an area of broken ground where rocky outcrops alternated with broom and dead bracken. Surely he must

have overrun his bird and picked up the scent of
another? On the other hand, it was just the sort
of cover for which a strong runner would head.
Anyway, if I called him off now we would have failed.
I waited.

Time went by. There was some chatting among
the onlookers. The judge began to fidget. He was going
to tell me to call my dog.

I saw movement at the edge of the cover. Ash
returned over the first fence. His chin was up. He was
holding a kicking pheasant clear of the ground. He
cleared the nearer ditch and struggled through the
hedge. There was a spontaneous round of applause as
he delivered the bird into my hand, sitting. The judge,
properly cautious, took the bird and parted the
feathers until he found the marks of pellets.

The light was fading and snowflakes were beginning to fall as we assembled in a Dutch barn. We
waited while the two judges debated. Joe glanced in
my direction while listening to the other judge who
was being vehement. My hopes rose. Joe, I guessed,
was hesitant, just because I was a friend, and wanted
to be persuaded.

Then he nodded and they gave their verdict. Ash
was placed first.

I shook hands all round and remembered to thank
the host and his keeper. I was glad to get back to the
car and gladder still when the engine's heat began to
warm the interior. I went back to the hotel for my
overnight bag and to call home from the payphone in
the hall. As well as confirming my continued health

and imminent return after a hot snack, I wanted to spread the glad tidings. But when Beth recognized my voice she said, 'Can't talk now. Tell me when you come,' and hung up.

If she could not even take time to ask how I was or even how we had got on, something had to be seriously wrong, but what? If the house had burned down, there would have been no phone for Beth to answer. I found more money and dialled again but the ringing tone went unanswered. Without waiting for a word with Joe, or even to give Ash his well-deserved dinner, I dived back into the car and set off for home.

The early dark of midwinter was aggravated by heavy clouds and before I reached the Forth Road Bridge the snow was coming down in earnest. Home-going traffic was slowed almost to a crawl but I carved my way through it with a display of downright bad manners which I hope never to have to repeat. Twice my lights seemed to be failing and I pulled off to wipe the packed snow off the glass. I saw several cars that had slid off into the countryside, one of them still surrounded by vehicles with flashing lights. My car was determined to go the same way, but I held it more or less straight by grit and willpower and turned in at the front gates of Three Oaks after a journey time which I would have considered dangerously brief on a summer Sunday afternoon. There were no emergency vehicles to be seen, the house was still standing, there was no sign of a fire and I could see movement behind the lit curtains. My worst imaginings abated.

To my further relief Beth, leading a sleepy Sam

with one hand and balancing a tray on the other, met me in the hall, shook her head and said, 'Hush!'

'It isn't Sam, is it?' I whispered.

She shook her head. 'Daffy had a bit of a shake-up,' she said softly. 'She's all right, more or less, but having a lie-down. Hannah came back – she hated it at home, with her father away most of the time – and she's sitting with Daffy now. Joe's been on the phone, in a tizzy because you'd vanished without a word and he didn't know whether you were unconscious in a ditch. I told him that you would be on the way home because I'd let you know that something was wrong, so it was my fault really. I was just going to brew more tea or something. Are you hungry?'

I thought about it and realized that I had got by on one sandwich and an apple since my early breakfast. 'Starving,' I said.

She nodded. 'Go and sit with Daffy. She can tell you her story, if she feels up to it. That'll let Hannah finish up.'

Hannah, drawn by our whispering or the sound of the car, emerged from the sitting room. She looked more alert and cheerful and I thought that the image of her Dougal might be slipping from reality into memory. I was still wondering why Daffy needed a sitter.

Before I could ask, Hannah said, 'How did Ash get on?' Not, you will note, how did her owner, trainer and handler get on? At Three Oaks, the dog was all-important. But at least she had remembered to ask.

'He's still in the car, and unfed,' I told her. I paused before adding, 'We won.'

Hannah beamed, stood on her toes and kissed me.

Beth looked pleased but only said, 'You're not going to crow over Isobel, are you?'

'Of course I am,' I said. 'That was my only reason for trying so hard.'

Beth made a face at me. 'Daffy won't go to hospital, won't speak to the police, won't eat or drink anything and she won't even let me call the doctor.' Beth combined a sigh with blowing a strand of hair away from her face. I tucked it back for her, took the tray from her and put in down on the hall table. 'Thanks. She says she doesn't want to be a nuisance! Well, she's a damn sight more nuisance worrying everybody sick. She just lies on the settee, moaning. See what you can do with her.'

Beth had to be seriously upset to let such *doubles entendres* slip by.

The sitting room, I found, was lit only by the firelight, supplemented by one small table lamp. Even that poor illumination seemed to be too much, because Daffy was stretched on the settee with a cloth over her eyes. She was wearing a dress which I seemed to recognize as one of Hannah's. She put up a listless hand to lift an edge of the cloth and peep at me. Sarda, sprawled across her lap, watched every movement with anxious eyes. 'It's you,' Daffy said hoarsely.

It was not the occasion for a funny answer, nor a pedantic one. 'It's me,' I confirmed, throwing grammar to the winds.

'How did you get on?'

'I thought nobody was going to ask. We got a first.'

'Well done! So Ash can go forward to open stakes.' The news would usually have had her on her feet. Instead, she sounded only mildly interested.

'What happened to you?' I asked her. 'Beth and Hannah are too busy to tell me anything. And I don't think that they know a lot.'

She roused slightly but remained prone. 'We packed up early because of the snow,' she said in a tired voice. 'Mrs Cunningham invited me to stay for a meal, but there was a heap of things waiting for me at home and now I had a chance to get at them at last and have the place clean and the laundry done before Rex comes home again. Am I making sense?' she asked.

'Perfect sense,' I assured her.

'I seem to be thinking through cotton wool. Mrs Cunningham offered to drive me home but conditions were rotten for driving and I thought that I'd probably be safer walking on the back road. Well, I set off to walk home. I had Sarda with me – on a lead, thank God! It was almost dark and snowing hard, but I had a good torch and good boots with plenty of tread, so we got along all right until we came to the place between the walls, you know where I mean?'

I said that I did. The cottage which Rex and Daffy shared was on a side-road that came off on the other side of the village, but an even more minor road, little more than a lane, cut the corner and would have saved her a mile. About half a mile from Three Oaks, the road squeezed between the high garden wall belonging to a farmhouse and a drystone wall to a field.

Daffy's voice was getting stronger. 'We were in the middle of that bit when a car arrived suddenly. It seemed to come out of nowhere. One moment it was dark, a moment later the world was full of blazing bright snowflakes and a pair of lamps was rushing at us. He couldn't have pulled up on the snow, even if he'd seen me in time, and you know how narrow the road is just there. The garden wall is impossibly high so I went the other way. I threw myself to the side of the road, dragging Sarda after me, couldn't stop and ended up doing a dive over the wall into the field. I don't know whether Sarda was dragged over on the lead or if she jumped but she seems all right. It was damn close, he actually hit the duffel bag which was over my shoulder. But there's a drop to the field and I came down on a big stone with Sarda on top of me. I was dazed and I seemed to have cut my head and it was nearer to come back here and anyway there wouldn't have been anyone at home. You don't mind?' she asked anxiously.

'Of course not,' I said. 'Don't be an ass. We'd have minded very much if you'd done anything else. Let's have a look at you.'

She peeped out from under the cloth again and evidently discovered that the light no longer hurt her eyes. She discarded the cloth – one of my scarves, I noticed – and sat up, tucking the skirt modestly under her knees. Marriage had certainly changed her. The change was mostly for the better but sometimes I missed the old, outrageous Daffy.

During my army days I had gained some experience of injuries. I put up the top light without causing more than a frown of discomfort and examined her. A lump like half an egg was lifting her hair above her right ear, but Beth had already cleaned up the attendant cut. Several other abrasions had been plastered. She was breathing normally and comfortably and, though stiff and sore, could move all her limbs. Her eyes looked normal. She was pale but not clammy. I judged that she had had a mild concussion but was already coming out of it.

I switched off the big light again and sat down. 'You'd better stay here overnight,' I said. 'Just in case you have any after-effects.'

'Mrs Cunningham already said that. And Hannah says that I can come in with her.'

'Good arrangement,' I said with relief. The spare bedroom now doubled as a nursery. If Daffy had slept there, Sam would have had to come in with us and he was a noisy and demanding roommate.

'It's very odd that you didn't see the car coming,' I said. 'He came from in front of you?'

'No, it came from behind. And you know how falling snow muffles noise.'

'Even so, there would have been a lot of light spilling forward and illuminating the snowflakes.'

Daffy rubbed her eyes. Her mind, usually bright, was working again. 'I didn't expect a car. You hardly ever see traffic on that road except a tractor or a small herd of cows. And I was thinking of other things. Partly I was wondering how you'd got on. Then again, it wasn't quite dark. And a lot of people prefer to use dipped headlights in fog or snow, so as not to make it reflect back in their eyes. He may have un-dipped the moment he saw me.'

'I suppose all that's true,' I said. 'You seem to have thought it out.'

'I've had nothing else to think about, lying here.'

'All the same, why don't you want the police?'

'What could they do?' she asked petulantly. 'Anyway, I was just as much at fault as he was. I should have been paying attention. And if I did call the police and they did manage to arrest somebody, he would probably turn out to be a friend or relation of somebody I know or somebody important and I'd be in for endless hassle. Sod's Law.'

It was certainly too late for the police to accomplish anything that night. The guilty vehicle would almost certainly be home and cold by now and much snow had fallen over the whole scene. Daffy's duffel bag was on the carpet beside her. There was a rip through which her spare jeans showed. I turned the bag in my hands. There were no convenient flakes of paint to be seen. 'We'll put this away in polythene,' I said, 'just in case. I can lend you another bag for the moment.'

Beth called me to come and take my meal. I decided to sleep on the problem.

*

There were no alarms in the night, but all the same I was restless. Daffy's accident fitted too neatly together with other events, to make a pattern which I did not want to recognize. It seemed to me that somebody might mean to do Daffy harm. The thought was not conducive to sound sleep under the same roof.

Daffy herself had slept well and was up early, hobbling around like an old lady but doing her share of the work, a still worried Sarda constantly at her heel. Daffy was showing several more lumps which had developed during the night and some bruises which had hardly been visible earlier had now blossomed into Glorious Technicolor, but I judged that any danger of serious injury or concussion was now gone. I was waiting in the kitchen when she and Hannah came in for breakfast, while Beth was getting Sam up and ready for the day.

'Think back,' I told Daffy. 'I know that you weren't paying attention at the time, but try to remember. Have you any idea what sort of a car it was?'

'None at all,' said Daffy. 'Just a big blur behind bright lamps.'

'Did it sound like a big car or a small car?'

Daffy thought back. 'Big,' she said at last.

She was probably right. The tear in her duffel bag had been up near the draw-cord and, knowing how Daffy carried the bag slung over her shoulder, almost certainly out of reach of a conventional family car. But there would be little to be gained by pursuing that line any further. Memory can record very erratically in moments of emergency. Once, in my youth, I was knocked off my bicycle by a large black car but my memory still insists that the culprit was a small red van.

'It came at you suddenly from behind. You were on your usual way home. I'll offer you two scenarios,' I told her, 'and you can pick the one that you think most nearly fits the circumstances. One, it was on a normal journey and you didn't see it or hear it until the driver upped his headlamps and was about to overtake you. Or, two, it was waiting in the driveway to the farmhouse until you passed by and then pulled out and followed you up. Which?'

Hannah was staring at me over her cereal but Daffy looked ready to cry. 'You're suggesting that somebody tried to run me down?'

'We have to consider it. What's more,' I said with sudden insight, 'I believe you've been wondering the same yourself but haven't wanted to recognize it.'

Daffy was shaking her honey-coloured head. 'I can't, I just *can't* believe that anyone hates me that much,' she whispered.

'If it's any comfort to you, I don't think it's anything personal. You're in somebody's way, that's all. Finish your breakfast.'

'Yes, of course.' Daffy opened her boiled egg and spread butter on a slice of toast. Her movements were abstracted. 'I'll give you this much,' she said. 'Before I got as far as the village, I saw the lights of a vehicle turn into the lane ahead of me. He could have gone ahead and stopped at the farmhouse gate and waited to see me coming.'

'Right. What's more,' I added, 'he doesn't necessarily want you dead. He hit your duffel bag. You carry
most of your worldly goods in that bag. He must have
thought that he'd hit you. And yet he didn't come
back. If he'd been innocent, or if he wanted you dead,
he'd certainly have come back.'

'He could have panicked and done a hit-and-run,'
Hannah piped up for the first time.

'Right again. All the same, my guess is that somebody wants Daffy out of action. We're going to have to
do something. His next move might be to poison all
the dogs, or something crazy like that.'

Beth came in, leading Sam. She heaved the child
onto his raised chair. Our discussion dried up. Beth
would have to be put in the picture but I was not
expressing my worries within Sam's hearing. When
Daffy had finished her breakfast, or at least had eaten
as much as we thought she needed, I got to my feet.
'Come on,' I said. 'We're going to Ardrossie,' I added to
Beth.

Beth, who looks so much less than her real age,
often surprises me by saying very little and then
proving to be far ahead of me. 'Yes, I think you'd
better,' she said. 'We don't want any more nonsenses.
But don't you think you'd do better to take the police
along?'

'Not at this stage,' I said pulling on my coat. 'We've
no proof of anything. But letting him know that we
know should stop him.'

Hannah was far behind but still pursuing. 'Just a

minute,' she said. 'Does this have anything to do with Dougal's disappearance?'

If I told her a lie now she would never forgive me. 'It might,' I admitted.

'Then I'm coming with you.' She grabbed her coat and followed us.

Beth came to the door. 'Don't do anything silly, any of you,' she said.

'Like what?' I asked her irritably. I had not paused to change my shoes for boots and I was slithering through several inches of snow at the time. The air had turned bitterly cold.

She looked over her shoulder to check on Sam. 'I don't know like what,' she said. 'But you usually manage to find something. I wish I could come with you.'

'Somebody has to mind the place and look after Sam,' I said. I had the engine running. I slammed my door and moved off before she could think of any more arguments.

The ploughs had been busy. The main roads were clear of snow but the sparse Sunday traffic threw up a spray of mingled slush and sand and I hated to think what the salt might be doing to the underside of my car. My companions wanted to ask questions but I shook my head. I was trying to think and to drive at the same time, which was more than enough to be going on with. The secondary road that led past Ardrossie had been snowed on since the plough had passed that way and the car wanted to play at being a carousel.

At Ardrossie, things were worse. I should have been warned when I saw Quentin Cove's big Shogun parked in a field gate off the farm-road, but I went on past the loading bay of the new buildings housing the dog-food factory, silent now in Sabbath calm. I pulled round the end and entered the spacious yard. On my right was the farm manager's cottage formerly occupied by Dougal Webb and to the left the back of the farmhouse.

I touched the brakes. Instantly, brakes and steering ceased to have any effect. Luckily I had entered the yard at a dead slow pace or I would shot straight into the open front of the big barn ahead of me and collided with a van or one of Quentin Cove's tractors, but at the last moment two wheels of the car passed from ice onto a narrow strip of frosted snow and we slewed to a halt and stalled. There was a silence, broken only by the sound of barking from the kennels behind the barn, before we began breathing again.

I found my voice. 'You two stay in the car,' I said firmly as I opened my door.

The source of all the ice was immediately evident. Quentin Cove, engulfed in oilskins, was crouched at the corner of the house, attempting a short-term repair with tape to a burst water-pipe. Onto the snow, which was already compacted by the passage of vehicles, water from the pipe was spraying and running across the surface, freezing as it went. The yard could well have doubled as a skating rink.

Forgetting that I was wearing smooth-soled shoes instead of my heavily treaded boots, I stepped out and almost went flat on my back. Somehow I managed to retain my balance. I had once been a moderately proficient skater and that half-forgotten skill, I think, saved me from going down. I remained upright, delicately poised, while without conscious effort or movement on my part I slithered slowly across the yard I came to a halt somewhere near the centre and stood still, hardly daring to breathe.

Quentin Cove had been watching my antics, in and out of the car. He heaved himself to his feet, scowling. 'What is it?' he asked me roughly. 'You can see I'm busy.'

'I want a word with you.'

'What word? I didn't think you came for the sight of my pretty face.'

I felt my temper beginning to slip. The farmer was acting as though he was the injured party. 'If I did,' I said, 'I'm doomed to bloody disappointment because you haven't got one.'

Chapter Eight

Quentin Cove hesitated. He took a second or two to decide whether to respond to my insult with amusement or aggression. His face had always been easy to read. I saw him review his options, make a conscious decision and summon up the adrenaline. I wondered for a moment whether, in my anger, I had gone too far. I was in no state to exchange blows with a doughty farmer. My only defence would be the unarmed combat that I had learned in the army. But nobody had taught me how not to kill. My mouth went dry.

He moved towards me with clenched fists and stepped straight onto the ice. But he did not have the knack of keeping still and staying balanced. Arms flailing and legs pedalling in all directions, he approached me so directly that I was sure disaster was imminent. But I managed to skate half a pace to the side and he passed me by so close that I had to duck under one of his flying arms. He slowed and came to a halt.

We were standing almost back to back a few yards apart. Cautiously, we both turned around.

It was not a propitious time to start a serious discussion, poised as it was on the very brink of farce, but I had to have a stab at it. I said, 'I came to pay a call on Mim. I like to assure myself that any dogs of my breeding are being well cared for. They're like family to me. May I see her, please?'

He pushed back the hood of his oilskin jacket. He was both surprised and perturbed. He had been expecting anything but that. 'No, you can't,' he snapped.

'That's what I thought,' I said. 'What I really came for was to tell you that we know what's been going on. So if Daffy – Mrs Mearns – meets with any more mishaps, we'll know who to blame and so will the police a few minutes later.'

His face flamed. 'I dinna ken whit you're on aboot,' he said, but I could see that my words had hit him hard. The one thing the lawbreaker fears is being found out. In his perturbation his speech had slipped back to its roots.

'Yes you do,' I said. 'You spiked Mrs Mearns' soft drink with vodka and then called the police to report her for drink-driving. But that didn't work and you knew that if she went on showing up at field trials she was bound to meet Mim at close quarters sooner or later. So last night, you callous bastard, you tried to run her down.'

He tried to look innocent and wronged but the expression did not sit well on his harsh features. 'Whit way would I dae a thing like that?' he demanded.

'If you want me to spell it out,' I said, 'you didn't want any of us to see Mim again, or at least not until

145

memories had faded. That's why you let my tyres down, to put me off coming to Lincraigs. But you particularly didn't want to go on bumping into Daffy at field trials, because she was the one person who would have realized that the dog you were running as Mim wasn't Mim at all.'

As I spoke, more and more facts and fragments of gossip fitted together and I was no longer guessing. Suddenly, I *knew*. 'You only acquired Mim,' I said, 'to get a legitimate pedigree and registration to switch to your own very similar and very talented bitch, daughter of the unplanned mating by Dorothy Hatton's dog. You couldn't even get the Hattons to acknowledge the breeding because their dog isn't registered and anyway other dogs had mated with yours before you got her back. On the other hand, assuming that it was Dorothy's dog that fathered your pup, Champion Clunie of Netherbrae figures in both pedigrees. You had a throwback to Clunie, very talented, strongly resembling Mim but ineligible to compete.'

'That means nothing,' he said. 'Nothing.'

'If you want to argue about it, we can always ask the police who tipped them off about Daffy – they don't usually act on anonymous tips. And although the breeding of Mim and of your bitch is similar it isn't identical. I still have a full sister of Mim. A DNA test would soon prove whether your bitch is one of that litter or not.'

As I finished speaking I suddenly saw the shape of another piece of the puzzle and I spoke out without giving myself time to think. 'What's more, I've only just figured out that that's what Dougal Webb was trying to blackmail me about. He thought that I was your partner in the fraud.' Another thought hit me. 'I bet he tried to blackmail you too, and that's why . . .' I left the remainder of the thought unspoken. It was beyond utterance. It might also be actionable.

He jerked, nearly slipped and only caught his balance by a wild wave of his arms. The fight went out of him and he looked ten years older. 'No,' he said hoarsely.

'You mean, that's not why?'

'I mean, I didn't! God, when you jump to conclusions you fairly cover the ground! We'll hae to enter you for the Grand National.'

I had forgotten the presence of Daffy and Hannah, and Quentin Cove had his back to them, but what I had been saying had not passed them by. While Hannah was still digesting my words, Daffy was out of the car. 'What did he do with Mim?' she cried. 'What did he do with poor Mim?' Something in her voice stabbed me through. I knew what it was like to love a dog.

'Can you produce her?' I asked him. He stood, silent. I think that he was too aware of his guilt, now that he was seeing it through the eyes of others, to protest any more. 'I'm sorry,' I said to Daffy.

'*He put her down? My darling Mim?*'

At the same moment, Hannah erupted from the other side of the car. 'He killed Dougal, isn't that what you're saying?'

Quentin Cove's voice went up an octave. 'Chrissake no! You can't land me with that!'

But his voice went unheeded. Whatever tension there might have been between the two kennel-maids at first, that had been years earlier when they were late teenagers. They were now friends and they had become used to working as a team. Their relationship had become almost telepathic. At this moment, it was as if they were a single organism with but one thought between them. Hannah had brought a heavy walking stick out of the car with her. Daffy, her stiffness marvellously cured for the moment, had emerged on the side nearer to the workbench in the barn and she grabbed a jack-handle out of the rack. They came at him together and they had the advantage of pushing off from the less slippery fringe of the yard. Gone were my two gentle helpers, who would brood over a sick puppy like mothers. These were two furies, hell-bent on revenge and caring for nobody.

Once they were on the ice they had to wave their arms for balance, adding menace to their advance. Seeing the weapons brandished by the advancing Valkyries, Quentin Cove paled. 'They've gone bloody mad,' he gasped. He tried to run, made no forward progress and ended up on his hands and knees. The tumble saved him for the moment. A swipe from Hannah passed over his head. The swing removed the last of her balance and she sat down heavily, still tobogganing on her rounded backside, while Daffy slid by, still upright but beyond swiping range.

Cove was right, of course. They had gone mad. I

could hardly blame them. Each believed that he had killed their loved one. But a successful blow from either weapon, especially the jack-handle, would result in endless complications and possibly the loss of a good kennel-maid. As Cove and Hannah struggled back to their feet I tried to place myself between him and the avenging harpies at whatever personal risk.

How long the dance, macabre yet farcical, went on I cannot guess. Probably only a matter of seconds although it seemed to be for an age that Cove was trying for his own front door, Hannah and Daffy were aiming to outflank him and I was struggling to stay between. I took a crack on the elbow from the jack-handle. Cove's luck held until the last second. A wild leap to avoid a swing from Daffy cost him his balance and he went down. As he struggled to rise, he took a great swipe from Hannah across his rounded bottom. The crack of it and his roar echoed around the farmyard and set the dogs barking again.

The mad pursuit was interrupted by the arrival of a small blue-and-white police car which crossed the yard in a well-controlled slide. The driver, I saw, was highly skilled. The car was nursed, at the very brink of control, into slowing and turning until it fetched up, parked neatly between my car and the mouth of the barn, without quite making contact with anything solid.

The driver's door opened and out stepped DCI Ewell's Sergeant, still immaculate in uniform and still looking far too young and pretty to be an officer. She needed only a glance to see who were the aggressors, who the defender and who was the intended victim and she launched herself valiantly in our direction. Some day I must find out what her shoes were soled with, because she kept her feet until the very last moment. Arriving and almost going past, she managed to grab Daffy's sleeve and the hood of Hannah's duffel coat. The jerk acted as the last straw to her balance and the three of them fell in a heap. Quentin Cove stood dumbstruck and so did I. Neither of us had seen quite so much leg before, except on a beach or in a chorus line.

The three began to pick themselves up while making themselves respectable and at the same time nursing bruised limbs. We were all breathing heavily. At some point the sun had come out and I found that I was sweating.

The Sergeant was the first to make it to her feet. With her hair flying, her cravat adrift and dark patches of wet marking her uniform, she looked less pretty and yet somehow much more desirable. 'You,' she said to Quentin Cove, 'had better go into your house and stay there.'

While the rest of us concentrated on catching our breaths, Cove nodded and set off for his door, adopting a skating action which seemed to meet the conditions. The burst pipe, I noticed, was still making its contribution to the water and ice. When he opened the door I could hear the drone of a vacuum cleaner. The door slammed and I heard the sound of the lock followed by two bolts. He was taking no risk of being followed inside by the kennel-maids from hell.

'Now,' said the Sergeant through clenched teeth, 'you three can come and sit in my car and explain yourselves.'

The idea of being cooped up in a very small car with so much angry young womanhood had no appeal for me. 'We'd have more room in my car,' I suggested. 'At least we would be in my own territory.'

The Sergeant nodded. 'Very well. But I'll take the driver's seat.'

'I was not going to drive off with you,' I said mildly.

The Sergeant was neither amused nor insulted. 'I like a steering-wheel to rest my notebook,' she said.

We slipped and slithered our ways back across the yard without disaster. Daffy and Hannah scurried into the rear, leaving me the front passenger seat. The Sergeant placed a small tape-recorder on the dash and pressed two keys. A tiny needle began to jump whenever we spoke. The Sergeant told the tape-recorder the date, time and place and who was present while repeating the information in her notebook. She also told the machine her name. She was, it seemed, Sergeant Bremner. 'Now,' she said, 'tell me what this was about.'

I decided that I had an equally interesting question to ask. 'Do you mind telling me how you come to be here?'

'I don't mind in the least. I'll even answer you. Mrs Cunningham phoned in. She felt that you might be under a misapprehension and that any possibility of hasty action should be nipped in the bud.'

The mention of misapprehension was interesting

but I decided to withhold comment until I knew a little more. 'Very sensible of her,' I said. Hannah and Daffy listened in silence while I explained the events of the last couple of days. The Sergeant listened intently while making an occasional note.

'There does seem to have been some jumping to conclusions,' the Sergeant said when I had finished. 'You make an interesting point about the substitution of dogs. You may be right in what you surmise about blackmail. But motive never makes a case. To leap from there to an assumption of murder—'

Hannah spoke up from behind me. 'Mr Cunningham never said anything about Mr Cove having murdered Dougal,' she said. 'I was the one who jumped to that conclusion.'

'I was going to say it, Hannah,' I said. 'But it seems that I was probably wrong. Mr Cove wasn't the only man your Dougal put the bite on.'

'I see.' Sergeant Bremner thought for a moment. 'I think I should tell you that your conclusions were, as you say, almost certainly wrong. We have not, as you seem to suppose, been sitting on our hands waiting for somebody like yourselves to do our jobs for us. Mr Little made a statement about witnessing the quarrel between Mr Cove and Mr Webb. He also stated that Mr Webb then drove off in a hurry. Mr Cove remained and supplied him with a bag of dog-meal. The transaction was hurried because Mr Cove was leaving to keep an appointment. That appointment was with six other men for drinks and a meal. They then went to a performance at the Byre Theatre. All this is heavily

vouched for. By the time that Mr Cove left his friends
and returned home, Miss Hopewell was already
worried about the disappearance of Mr Webb and was
actually waiting right here, where she remained until
around four a.m.'

'But—' Hannah began.

'It's my turn to jump to conclusions,' the Sergeant
said firmly, 'because I can guess what you want to say.
And yes, it's possible to come up with several scenarios
in which Mr Cove might have done mischief to Mr
Webb. It's possible, for instance, that Mr Webb had
gone off on some errand of his own about which we
know nothing, forgetting his date with Miss Hopewell
or else just plain standing her up. He could then have
returned after she left here, roused his employer from
his bed – just before dawn – resumed the quarrel and
the rest followed. But that all seems very improbable
and since we don't yet have confirmation that the
body in the bonfire was that of Mr Webb, there seems
little point discussing it.'

'I accept that,' Hannah said in a very small voice.
'But there's one thing I must know. Was Dougal really
a blackmailer?'

Glancing sideways I saw that the Sergeant had
written the word *was* in longhand and capitals and put
a box round it. 'I'm afraid so,' she said. 'We've come
across several instances that fall within the definition.
He was too cautious to make a direct demand for
money or money's-worth with menaces, but we now
know that when he took a fancy to some valuable
personal item he was not above making oblique threats

in order to drive home a very hard bargain. He may even have convinced himself that using knowledge to gain better terms was an acceptable business practice. That, I suppose, could have furnished any number of motives for his murder. On the other hand, it would equally give Mr Webb a motive for disappearing, if he knew that his misdeeds were coming to light.'

'Is that how he acquired the Lotus?' I asked her.

'You can't seriously expect me to tell you that. But, Miss Hopewell,' she added over her shoulder, 'if you are now thinking of blaming yourself on the grounds that he took to blackmail in order to finance his court-ship of you and your possible future together, you can put it firmly out of your mind. He set out on that path before you and he had even met.'

I decided that Sergeant Bremner was a perceptive and humane young woman, undoubtedly destined for high rank. I added those labels to several others which I had mentally attached to her.

'Thank you,' Hannah whispered. 'I'll remember that.'

'That's all very well,' Daffy said suddenly, 'but we haven't dealt with the matter of the dog.'

'We're going to deal with it now,' said the Sergeant. She used the driving mirror to tidy herself further. 'Come with me, Mr Cunningham. You two, wait there, please.'

We made our way cautiously around the edge of the yard. As we did so, the spray of water leaking past the bandage on the fractured pipe diminished and stopped. The Sergeant knocked on the door. After some clattering of locks and bolts, it was opened by Mrs Dundee. She was very businesslike in a floral pinny and plastic gloves, with a large duster in her hand and a smell of polish wafting around her. 'He's below,' she said with great formality. 'Who'll I say is after him?'

'The police,' said the Sergeant. Then, noticing the unfortunate combination of phrasing, she added quickly, 'I'm not after him, I just want a quick word with him.'

Mrs Dundee stood aside as Quentin Cove came up through a trapdoor, rather like a pantomime Demon King in slow motion. He had removed his waterproofs and was in dusty overalls. 'Hell of a place to put a stopcock,' he said angrily. 'But that'll have to stay off until the plumber comes. And God knows when that'll be – half the pipes in the kingdom have burst. You'd better come in. You can carry on upstairs,' he added to Mrs Dundee. 'Don't run any water without speaking to me first.'

He led us into a shabby sitting room which smelt of mingled dust and polish. We took stuffed chairs which had sagged over the years into comfortable shapes. It was warm in the central heating and I took off my coat.

Cove shrugged out of his bib-and-braces dungarees and took his own chair. 'I don't know what this bugger's been saying,' he began.

'Then we'll let him go over it again,' the Sergeant said. She went through the same drill of briefing her tape-recorder and simultaneously making notes. Then she glanced at me. 'Now.'

'Your farm manager, Dougal Webb,' I told Cove, 'made an attempt to blackmail me. At the time I couldn't think what he was hinting at, but he seemed to think that mention of the Kennel Club would put the fear of God into me.' For the sake of the record, I decided to spell it out clearly. 'Then other things began to add up. You were very keen to buy Mim, a seriously gun-shy pup, from Mrs Daffodil Mearns, one of my kennel-maids, but when she encountered you with Mim at a novice trial, which you won, there was no sign of gun-shyness. As far as I know, there's no cure for gun-shyness.'

Cove sneered. 'That only goes to show that I'm a better trainer than you are.'

I refused to be needled. 'Maybe,' I said. 'But you were very careful to keep Mim away from Daffy at the time. On her way home, Daffy went into a pub with Mrs Kitts. You arrived on their heels and bought Daffy the soft drink that she wanted. That drink was spiked and somebody phoned the police to say that she was drinking and driving. They were stopped and Daffy was breathalysed, but she was just within the legal limit. Last night, Daffy was nearly run down by a vehicle in the dark and snow. To top it all, you stopped me coming to your farm after the rabbits, on the grounds that you'd let the rough-shooting to somebody else although there's no sign of a shooting tenant and you told Joe Little that he could come onto your land. While I was at the farm next door, my tyres were let down. It all adds up to the fact that you don't want anybody who knew Mim to meet up with her again.

'You may be able to suggest any number of explanations for this combination of facts. I can think of only one. I know that your neighbour's springer covered one of your bitches some time ago. His dog isn't registered, so none of the pups could be registered nor any of their descendants to infinity. You were giving the pups away for peanuts. But I think you kept one to train as a worker and that she turned out to be brilliant. You're a well-to-do farmer without many worlds left to conquer. Your one unfulfilled ambition has been to make a name for yourself in field trials. So you were desperate to go trialling with your bitch, but only pedigreed pups can be registered and only registered dogs can be entered.

'Then you saw Mim. She was brindled, a throwback to Champion Clunie of Netherbrac, as was your young bitch. They looked identical. The difference was that Mim was registered and had a good pedigree. You tried to buy Mim. A little later when she turned out to be gun-shy, Daffy sold her to you on the understanding that she would be going to a good home. But that isn't Mim that you won the novice stake with and were so desperate to enter in an open stake last week. That's your own bitch.'

Quentin Cove had listened in silence but with a growing expression of injured innocence. When I halted, he stared at me for a few seconds and then said, 'You're daft as a brush. And you canna prove a word of it.'

'But can you disprove a word of it?' I asked him. 'Bring out your bitch and see if she recognizes Daffy. Give us a clump of hair for DNA testing.'

'I've no need to disprove a damn thing,' he retorted. 'It's your story, it's for you to prove it. What's more, there's no law against changing a dog's name.'

'Fraud and false pretences,' I told him.

Sergeant Bremner looked up and frowned. 'I don't see the Procurator Fiscal making a case out of it,' she said. 'There's no big money involved.'

'It runs to big money in the long run,' I told her. 'And I've no need to prove it,' I said to Cove. 'I've done what I came to do, which was to make sure that if anything else happened to Daffy or to us you'd find yourself being looked at damned hard by the police. And if you attempt to enter that bitch in competition again I'll make a report to the Kennel Club. They'll certainly insist on DNA testing.'

That threat shook him as nothing else had. 'Ah, now, there's no call for the likes of that,' he said quickly. 'You've said yourself, many a time, that the Kennel Club rules were a to hell!'

'I don't think I put it quite like that,' I said.

'Damn near it. I've heard you tell a committee member to his face that if their closed gene-pool policy had been in force in the old days we'd never have had half our present breeds. You said – and I remember it well – that the German shorthaired pointer was virtually the only breed to produce dual champions, show-bench and field trial, in the last twenty years and that the breed came about as a mishmash of Spanish pointer, German pointer and the foxhound.'

'And the Hanoverian Schweisshund. Don't forget that one,' I said mildly. I was rather flattered that he should have remembered my words so accurately. I pulled myself together. 'All this has damn all to do with the case. Under the rules as they are, however little I agree with them, you've been robbing other competitors of the rewards they're entitled to. In fact, come to think of it, you've robbed me. And because my dog did not get the award it had earned, its value and the value of its progeny to infinity may be diminished. You're an amateur, but competition success is my bread and butter and you stole it from me.'

'I'll fight you. I'll fight every inch o the way,' he said furiously.

'You can try,' I said. 'I think you'll find that the odds are against you. And there's one other thing. We'll have to buy our dog-food somewhere else from now on.'

He thought it over for some seconds before it sank in. 'Damn it to hell, there's nae need for that,' he exploded. 'I'd not do sic a thing, ye ken that fine.'

'I'm sorry, Quentin,' I said. 'But you *did* do something *just* like that. Or can you still produce Mim alive?'

His eyes slid away from mine. I got to my feet and picked up my coat. 'You won't be proceeding against the girls?' I asked the Sergeant.

'I must make a report. I won't recommend action.'

'Hey!' Cove said. 'Those wee buggers laid into me, in my own yard!'

'Then you'd better show the Sergeant your bruises,' I told him. I left the room, fairly confident that, protected as he had been by his oilskins, his only bruises would be to his ego.

In the hall, Mrs Dundee's small bottom was presented to me as she worked her way backwards down the stairs, dusting and polishing the exposed woodwork as she came. I only recognized her when she straightened up, glad of any excuse to stop for a rest and a chat. 'It's yourself,' she informed me. She looked more cheerful than when I had seen her last. She was no more beautiful a sight but at least her hollow cheeks seemed to have filled out a little and her cheery grin somehow seemed to justify her over-large mouth.

'Hello,' I said. 'I didn't know that you worked for Mr Cove.'

She seated herself comfortably on the fifth or sixth tread, her gnarled face on a level with mine. 'Och, for years he was asking me to come, but I was well enough, doing half days for Mrs Macevoy and efterneens up at the Big Hoose. I couldna come here while yon skellum Dougal Webb was around the place. But then Mrs Macevoy turned me awa, just acause she couldna put her hand on a wee bit jewellery I dinna mind ever seeing. And just then Mr Webb disappears like snow off a dyke. Then Jack Gilchrist told Mr

Cove I was free an he asked me again. And no afore time. Goad, the dust that was in the place!'

'What did you have against Dougal Webb?' I asked her. Surely he could never have been blackmailing such a poor creature.

'He had a way wi him but I found he wisna suithfast. There was a thing he wheedled out o me, in confidence like, and then let oot the poother. But it wasna just that. Sir Ian Bewlay hissel told me to steer clear of Mr Webb. I get my wee cottage from Sir Ian in return for my two hours in the efterneen and I'd no want to be put oot in the road for bein gran billies wi the likes of Dougal Webb.'

'Sir Ian wouldn't put you out just for that, would he?' I asked.

'He seemed awfu positive when he spoke to me. "You stay clear of yon man Webb," he said to me. "There's bad blood there," he said, "and if you want to keep what's yours," he said, "you'll gie him a wide berth."' Mrs Dundee paused. Something was missing. 'He said,' she added suddenly.

'It was good advice,' I said, 'though he may not have meant it quite the way you took it. Would you come out to my car for a minute? There's something I want to ask you and I don't want to be interrupted.' I nodded towards the sitting room door. Voices were being raised. I gathered that the Sergeant was giving Quentin Cove a hard time on the subject of where he and his car had been, around dusk of the previous day.

She looked doubtfully at me and then shrugged and came along. 'My time's amost up,' she said. It was like walking with a child, but she might have taken it amiss if I had held her hand to steady her until we were on a good surface. Instead, I stooped and let her take my arm. She hopped cheerfully up into the front passenger's seat and exchanged greetings with the two in the back. Daffy and she seemed to know each other of old. I got into the driver's seat – with some difficulty because the Sergeant had parked uncomfortably close to my door. I started the engine to put a little warmth into the heater.

'You know that we found a body, just after you spoke to us that Saturday?' I said. 'And you know that the body may have been Dougal Webb?'

She nodded in answer to each question.

'It's important to find out who had a reason to dislike Mr Webb. I think you should tell us why Sir Ian had a grudge against him. Unless you've already told the police?' Mrs Dundee paled. 'I'll see that you don't suffer for it,' I added, 'and if it turns out to be irrelevant, neither the police nor Sir Ian need never know.'

'I canna be sure,' she said.

'But it began just after Dougal Webb betrayed your trust?'

She nodded again.

Daffy leaned forward so that her hair tickled my cheek. 'Mrs Dundee,' she said, 'was it anything to do with your Jimmy?'

The car moved slightly on its springs as Mrs
Dundee jerked. 'Maybe,' she said. 'It might.'

'There have been whispers going around for years,'
Daffy said. 'Mrs Dundee, is Sir Ian Jimmy's dad?'

Mrs Dundee uttered a pained cry. I could feel her
small frame shaking in the seat next to me. There
were tears on her sallow cheeks. Then the dam burst
and the story came tumbling out.

The sun was melting the surface of the ice, giving it a
fresh polish and doing away with the last traces of
grip. When Mrs Dundee had finished I got out of the
car with some difficulty and escorted her back to
the house, although she had less far to fall than any
of us. Returning, I was faced again with the task of
squeezing in through a narrow gap. In a moment
of frustration I put my bottom against the Sergeant's
car and pushed. On that melting ice and aided by a
distinct slope, the car slid easily. Without further help
from me, it travelled several yards sideways. I flinched,
expecting at any moment to hear the crumpling sound
as the front hit a stanchion supporting the head of the
open front of the barn or the back struck the workbench. But the car, as though guided by a mighty hand,
arrived between the two with an inch to spare at either
end. And there it stopped.

The Sergeant was going to need help, and a lot of
it, to get her car out of there and I doubted whether
she would get it from Quentin Cove. But I had rather
modified my favourable view of Sergeant Bremner

since she and I had failed to see eye to eye on the subject of whether blocking the advancement of one of my dogs by deception had constituted a fraud. I coaxed my car gently across the yard and hurried away.

Chapter Nine

If, as I said earlier, God created spaniels and sponges on the same day, He knocked off after that and played snowballs. A short-haired dog like a Labrador can come in out of the snow almost bone dry, but take a small spaniel out in deep, fresh snow and it will come home like the makings for a Christmas tree, with a snowball dangling from each lock of hair. Any attempt to remove those snowballs by hand turns them into chunks of ice locked fast to the hairs.

Dogs need free-running exercise. That is one of the few incontrovertible facts in the canine world. As the snow continued, novice and open stakes were being cancelled or postponed all around; but, when the thaw came, honours would go to those who had managed to keep their dogs fit and up to the mark. Training and walking had to continue. We tried hard to stick mainly to a long strip of field which a dense wood of pine and Scots fir had sheltered from the prevailing wind, but a fresh fall of snow came in on a different wind and after that each spaniel (and other hairy breeds residing with us as boarders) had to be thawed as well as dried in the blow-drying chamber which had been created from what had once been a lean-to privy, then brushed into an unmatted state and with luck returned to its kennel without picking up a fresh cargo of Christmas decorations.

Isobel was still confined to her bed – or else, knowing what life would be like at Three Oaks, she had decided to hibernate until the spring. Henry spared us what time he could, but he had his own life to lead in addition to tending a 'flu-ridden wife.

All this is merely to explain that for the next few days we were very busy indeed. I managed to give Beth a detailed account of our visit to Ardrossie, but we never seemed able to sit down at the same time long enough for a serious discussion and, to be honest, I was thoroughly sick of the subject anyway. Even Hannah seemed to have put it out of her mind. The revelation of defects in her lover's character seemed to have turned a grand tragedy into a passing disappointment. She was pulling her weight again and even singing occasionally. The church saw much less of her.

It was Beth's custom to go into Cupar on a Thursday morning to do the week's shopping, accompanied by any of us who was in need of a visit to the shops, the library or the dentist. That week, Jenny had stepped on a fragment of broken glass and cut one of her pads. Despite my ministrations, the cut was slow to heal. Isobel would certainly have got out of bed to attend to it, possibly ruining her own health in the process, so we kept the news from her, swearing Henry to secrecy, and Jenny and I joined the trip to Cupar. At the last moment Henry, whose car had gone in for servicing, decided to leave Isobel's care to a helpful neighbour and come with us.

It was Beth's journey, so she drove. She parked behind the big supermarket. She and Henry hurried inside while I led Jenny, limping bravely, through the store and along the pavement to the surgery.

The vet and Isobel had at one time been colleagues. He was a born gossip and the disinfecting and stitching of Jenny's pad was accompanied by enquiries after Isobel's health and the recitation of many recipes for the relief of 'flu symptoms, ranging from herbal through homoeopathy to folk remedies verging on witchcraft and totally unsuitable for a man of science. He replaced my amateurish bandage with a more professional version and charged me an arm and a leg.

Jenny, always a good patient, was quite unmoved by all the attention but by the time we neared our car again her better foreleg had tired and she was limping pathetically. But that fact cut no ice with a big man who arrived from behind us and thrust past to reach the door of his Isuzu Trooper, so nearly treading on Jenny's bad foot that she yipped in fear.

Instead of looking round, the man back-heeled viciously, catching her in the ribs. 'Bloody dogs!' he said.

Then he turned and I saw that he was Sir Ian Bewlay.

I had no wish to quarrel with one of the larger landowners in the area and thereby lose a valuable outlet for dog-training. Jenny was hurt but not injured. On the other hand, although I am not aggressive by nature, nobody, but nobody, kicks one of my dogs without repercussions. I began to seethe.

'Don't you dare to do that again,' I said. I was further annoyed to find that my voice was hoarse.

He turned and looked down at me from his considerable height. I saw him recognize me and decide that I was a person of no account, dust beneath his wheels. Large though he was, I thought that he looked soft. My training in unarmed combat had been years earlier but it had been thorough. There were witnesses not far away. If I could provoke him into lashing out, I was sure that I could damage him with impunity.

'Do what?' he sneered.

I pointed down at Jenny, who had retired behind my legs and was peering past, wondering what was going on. People, in her experience, just did not behave like that. 'You kicked my dog,' I said.

'So I did. What do you want me to do? Kiss it better?'

'You could start by apologizing. Tell the dog you're sorry. Give her a pat. Then we'll take it from there.'

Timothy Pratt, Sir Ian's shadow and sycophant, pushed forward. 'Who do you think you're talking to?' he demanded.

'I think I'm talking to the mannerless boor who kicked my dog,' I retorted, 'and I'm still waiting for him to say that he's sorry.' I shifted my weight onto the balls of my feet, ready to counter any sudden moves.

Sir Ian glanced around the car park, then weighed me up. My appearance may be fragile but my readiness must have shown. He broke off eye contact. 'But I'm not sorry,' he mumbled. He turned away quickly and climbed into his vehicle – leaving me frustrated but taking with him, I was pleased to note, most of a large dog-turd which Jenny had deposited in the excitement of the confrontation.

'But you will be sorry,' I promised him silently as he pulled away.

I put Jenny into the car. The rush of adrenaline had left my mouth dry and I needed a drink. But first, while my dander was still up, I wanted to fire the first shot in my battle against Sir Ian Bewlay. I needed to commit myself before my temper cooled.

The nearest public telephones were inside the supermarket. As I placed my call, I could see Beth and Henry working their way towards the checkout. Kirkcaldy answered. I asked for Detective Inspector Ewell but he was out, of course. Then, unexpectedly, the voice became helpful. Where was I calling from? It turned out that DI Ewell was not far away. I suggested that he might care to join me for coffee in one of the local hotels. There was a pause while Ewell was consulted over the radio, during which I spotted another familiar face. Then the voice told me that he would be there in ten minutes.

Beth and Henry were emerging from the checkout, putting away their credit cards. At the long worktop provided by a thoughtful management (and why can't others follow suit?) I helped Beth to transfer her shopping from a trolley into several cardboard cartons. Henry trans-shipped his own more modest purchases.

I could feel Beth glancing at me. She knew that something was wrong. As much to distract her as for any other reason, I said, 'That was Mrs Macevoy behind you in the queue.'

Beth turned and stared at Mrs Macevoy's departing back. 'The fat ginger-headed tart? I wondered who she was.'

'Do you fancy coffee?' I asked her. 'Because I've made a date to meet Mr Ewell for coffee in a few minutes.'

'Yes,' Beth said slowly, 'I think that's a very good idea.'

Mrs Macevoy, as we reached the car park, was driving off in a nearly new BMW, custom-painted an unusual colour which I can only liken to that of a nearly ripe plum or the underside of a red snooker ball which is reflecting the green cloth.

We loaded the cartons of shopping onto the back seat of our car, well out of Jenny's reach but still managing to leave room for Henry. Jenny was not given to stealing food, but the habit is easily learned and difficult to eradicate. For the moment, we left the car where it was, the supermarket being better provided with parking than the hotel. It was a five-minute walk between the two and Beth said not a word. Either she was coming down with Isobel's 'flu or something that she had seen or heard had set her thinking. I wondered whether to interrupt her thoughts by telling them both about Sir Ian's arrogance and my determination to hit back; but Beth would either have told me to cool off or else she would have gone to war on my behalf.

The Detective Inspector joined us as the waitress brought coffee. I had asked for a pot and five cups, but I was relieved to see that he was not for once accompanied by the alluring Sergeant Bremner. If the Sergeant was not aware that I had helped her car into its absurd predicament, she would certainly have guessed that I had had a quiet laugh at her expense.

Ewell accepted a cup (black, no sugar) and then looked at me with eyebrows raised. I glanced round but we had the lounge to ourselves except for a group of middle-aged women in the furthest corner, all talking shrilly and simultaneously. There was no danger of being overheard.

'Has the identity of the body been confirmed?' I asked.

Ewell hesitated and then shrugged. 'In confidence? It has and it hasn't. We have the report on the DNA tests. Of course, the body was partially cooked over a long period. The lab did what they could. They found a partial match with DNA obtained from hairs out of his hairbrush, but not enough for a court of law. They say that discrepancies were only to be expected. Now, what were you going to tell me?'

'I don't know how many of Dougal Webb's blackmail victims you've traced—' I began.

'One or two,' he said. 'One or two.'

'— but do you know about Sir Ian Bewlay?'

His eyebrows, which had come down, shot straight up again and stayed there. 'What about Sir Ian?'

'Do you know Mrs Dundee?'

'What does she have to do with anything?'

I decided that we had asked each other enough questions for the moment. 'She can tell you a story.'

'You tell me,' he said. 'Mrs Dundee – if you mean the old lady in the cottage near Gifford Hill – has been interviewed but she told us nothing of interest. I'd rather know what you make of her.'

'All right,' I said. 'Here goes. About twenty years ago, Mrs Dundee was housemaid at Marksmuir House. Sir Ian seduced her – or, if you credit her story, forced himself on her. When it comes to lairds and house-maids, the dividing line can be nebulous. She bore him a son.'

'A common enough story,' Ewell said.

'Here comes the uncommon bit. He never denied paternity. He couldn't. Apparently there were several witnesses to the deed because it happened on the dining table just after a boozy lunch party.'

I paused and for a moment there was silence between us. Then Beth said, 'That's awful!'

'You may – or may not – think that what followed was worse. While she was unable to work, believe it or not, he stopped her wages. Afterwards, he paid her the minimum required by law for child maintenance until the boy came of age and he let her stay in the cottage in return for two hours' work every afternoon. She had to go out cleaning in the mornings to make ends meet and even so she must have had a thin time. After she lost her other job with Mrs Macevoy she was almost starving. When we saw her, the day we found the body, she was picking over the fields for forgotten vegetables in order to stay alive while she waited for her son to come home. He's an apprentice in the merchant navy. She begged a few rabbits off us, that day. She won't take Assistance – she thinks of it as charity.'

Beth was looking astonished, as well she might, but not for the reason I expected. 'Mrs Macevoy sacked her?' she exclaimed.

'Yes. Apparently Mrs Macevoy suspected her of stealing some piece of jewellery. My own impression is that Mrs Dundee would be the more honest of the two of them. I suspect that her only deception in her life was in assuming the title of Mrs when she had the child. She's never been married. But that's by the way.

'A year or so ago, Webb pretended to be very sympathetic and coaxed her story out of her. Soon afterwards, Sir Ian told her to stay well away from Webb, on pain of losing her cottage. Around that time, Webb suddenly sported a very expensive wristwatch resembling one which I had seen and envied on Sir Ian, who still wears a Rolex but of a slightly different pattern. That would make Sir Ian very unhappy. He's a man who prefers every penny to work for him and nobody else.

'I think we can take it that Webb wasted no time before putting the bite on him and acquiring Sir Ian's Rolex at a bargain price. You can imagine how the story would have looked in the gutter press. She must be twenty years older than he is and she can never have been a beauty, besides hardly coming up to his navel. Imagine their photographs side by side along with the story of how shabbily he's treated the mother of his son. His parliamentary ambitions would have gone right up in smoke.'

'I'm surprised she accepted it,' Ewell said. 'The days are past when a landlord can behave like that. The law would have protected her. For one thing, it would never have allowed him to turn her out of her cottage.'

Henry had been listening attentively. 'She's feudal,' he said. 'I thought so when we met her on the hill. To her, he's the laird and therefore omnipotent. His whims are acts of God. If she falls on hard times, that's fate. You find them like that sometimes in the country.'

Ewell shook his head unhappily. 'That's so. The attitude gets handed down from generation to generation. He was very high-and-mighty when we interviewed him. He didn't know a thing and seemed to be insulted that we thought he might. I'll tell you this much – I'm not looking forward to confronting him again.'

'Then don't,' said Beth.

'I must.' Ewell smiled grimly. 'Of all the people with a connection to Dougal Webb, he's the only one we've spoken to who has refused to account for his whereabouts between the time when Webb was last seen alive and the latest probable time of death.'

'In your shoes,' Henry said, 'I would leave that interview to your superintendent. It's more his job than yours.'

Ewell looked a little happier.

'You haven't exhausted the other possibilities yet,' I said. 'Did you ever find out where the Lotus came from?'

'Miles away,' Ewell said. 'Tracing ownership was easy. Apparently it was a cash deal and the previous owner, a Mr Pratt, claims to have received a satisfactory price.'

'Well I, for one, do not believe it,' said Henry. 'I can't see a salaried farm manager, especially one as thrifty as Dougal Webb, forking out the going price of a nearly new, expensive car totally unsuited to life on the farm. I take it that the seller was "Sanctimonious" Pratt?'

Ewell's mouth fell open. 'You mean Mr Timothy Pratt, the would-be councillor? I never connected the names. He lives outside Fife and Kinross, so the enquiry was conducted for us by the Tayside Force.'

'And is buddies with Sir Ian,' Henry said.

'He gets up on his soapbox for animal welfare,' I said. 'But he shot his own dog up the backside quite deliberately, to teach it a lesson. He only meant it to sting but he hopelessly misjudged the range. That was on one of Sir Ian's shoots, where Webb was commonly a beater.'

'You've stolen my thunder as usual,' Henry grumbled. 'I intended to spill those particular beans myself. I was at Three Oaks when he brought the poor beast to my wife, howling miserably – the dog, Inspector, not the Pratt. The damage was so bad that she had to castrate the poor beast. Imagine how

175

that would look to the animal lovers whose votes he's canvassing.'

Detective Inspector Ewell sighed heavily. 'That will be another uncomfortable interview. If I land Superintendent Aicheson with the interrogation of two members of the Establishment, I will not be popular.'

Beth had an anxious expression, which gave her the look of a pretty teenager. 'Accepting that,' she said, 'there's somewhere else you should look first. Why do you suppose Mrs Macevoy suddenly dispensed with the services of Mrs Dundee?'

'According to Mrs Dundee, Mrs Macevoy said that a piece of jewellery had gone missing,' I reminded her.

'And you said that you didn't believe it.'

'I did and I don't.'

'Well, then.'

Detective Inspector Ewell frowned. 'She never reported any such thing to the police.'

'Because it never happened,' Beth said firmly. 'John pointed Mrs Macevoy out to me in the supermarket just now. I've seen her in there in the past, without knowing who she was. She was always doing the typical shopping of a woman living alone. I rather envied her.'

I was startled. 'You envied her living alone?'

Beth laughed and patted my hand. 'No, you idiot! I envied her being able to do her shopping in a basket instead of a trolley, buying convenience foods instead of joints and sausages and eggs and bacon and vegetables by the ton and . . . and . . .'

'All right,' I said. 'I get the message.'

'But I get the messages. Today, her shopping wasn't as big as mine but it was much bigger than usual.'

'Maybe she was doing two weeks' shopping in one. Or stocking up for a visitor.'

'She was shopping for a man,' Beth said. 'Steaks and things. And beer and cigars. I've never seen her buy any of those before.'

Detective Inspector Ewell had literally jumped in his chair. 'She touched a nerve?' I asked him.

'She certainly did.' Ewell looked from Beth to me and back again. 'This is no secret – it just hasn't hit the media up here yet. Mrs Macevoy's husband was jailed in England, because that's where the rape took place. He was sent to Parkhurst. For some stupid administrative reason, the only address they had for him was the hotel where he'd been staying when it happened. So word has only just reached us.

'Apparently he lost his remission because he took part – a small part – in a riot in which a prison officer was injured. He was going to have to serve out his time, which would mean several more years. So he absconded from a working party. They thought that they had him bottled in the Isle of Wight. Then he was supposed to have been seen in Kent and again on a Channel ferry. Only when that lead turned out to be false were all Forces circulated and even then it took us a few days to make the connection with a local resident.'

'Now they tell you,' I said.

'Exactly.'

The group of women seemed to have left. We had

the lounge to ourselves. There was a silence while we assimilated the addition of a new character into the shifting scene.

'In that case, there's something else you should be thinking about,' Beth said at last. She looked bashfully at the Detective Inspector. 'You don't mind my making these suggestions?'

Ewell shook his head dumbly.

'It's nothing very hard and fast, just a pointer. When John was telling me about going to Ardrossie last Sunday, he said that Mr Cove was hunting under the floor for the stopcock.'

'Nothing very odd about that,' Henry said. 'In an old house, floors get relaid and the access hatch ends up in a different place, miles from the stopcock, which may not be needed for years at a time.'

'I know all that,' Beth said impatiently. 'I do know about old houses. I've never lived in any other kind. But John said that when he came up from under the floor he was all dusty with dried earth.'

I wondered where on earth (or in it) she was leading us. 'In an old house, the solum – the ground under the hung floor – isn't usually covered. It's just bare earth,' I explained. 'It gets very dry.'

'I wish you'd both stop interrupting,' Beth snapped. 'You keep telling me things I've known for years and making me forget what I was going to say next. Where was I?'

'You were saying that Mr Cove was dusty,' said Ewell. He still did not quite smile but there was a glint of amusement in his eye.

'Yes. And when John told me that, I had a sudden sense of – what do you call it? – déjà vu. I remembered Dougal Webb coming to deliver dog-food and standing in our doorway. For once, he'd come in his farming clothes instead of dressing up for Hannah's benefit, and his clothes were dusty with dry earth.'

'Farmers do get dirty,' I said.

'You're interrupting again,' Beth said severely. 'It had just thawed and the ground was very wet and muddy. But it was definitely earth, not barn dust or chaff. I thought he must have been digging in an out-building or something like that. But Mr Macevoy, when he was jailed, was also under suspicion of embezzling from the firm he worked for. None of the money ever turned up. And Dougal always seemed more flush with money than he should have been. He dropped hints about a legacy but nobody seems to know of any other relatives than the Macevoys.' She glared at me. 'And before you think you have to remind me that he was a blackmailer, let me point out that we don't know of a single occasion when he asked for money.'

'He was too careful for that,' Ewell said. 'He preferred to force people to sell him valuable things at silly prices. Very difficult to argue about afterwards – a bargain being a bargain under Scots law, silly or not. He probably saw nothing wrong in what he was doing, using leverage to get a better bargain. He may have felt that it was no more than an extension of normal business practice.'

'Which it is, of course,' said Henry.

'Not a defence which would stand up in court,' the

Detective Inspector said. 'Adding it all together, what Mrs Cunningham is suggesting is that Mr Macevoy had hidden his hoard under the floorboards at Gifford House and his nephew found it or knew that it was there.'

Beth was nodding. 'He was good at wheedling secrets out of people.'

'But it fits very well,' Ewell said. He sounded slightly indignant, as though Beth had no right to precede him to logical conclusions. 'It even fits with some bits and pieces that you don't know. I'll set it out and you can tell me if I'm assembling it wrongly.

'We've been watching for Mr Macevoy at roads and railway stations. He may have been home before we knew that he was loose. When Mrs Macevoy was interviewed, after the body was found, she gave the officers a tour of the house. They really only wanted to visit the kitchen to see whether any knives were obviously missing, but she had non-matching knives collected over the years, not a matching set. She swore that none was missing and it was impossible to be sure, one way or the other. She almost dragged the officers round the whole place. She said that the finding of a body had made her nervous and she wanted them to make sure that no villains were lurking ready to jump out at her, would you believe? She put on a good show. They reported that there was no sign of a visitor. He was probably under the floorboards all the time. That's what threw us off the scent. If she put down the carpet after he hid, the officers would ignore the underfloor space. They were looking for an unwelcome intruder

180

who couldn't have pulled the carpet back once he was under the floor.

'So it would seem that Macevoy arrived home, found that his nephew had been dipping into his hoard, killed him and put the body under the bonfire, ready for cremation when the foresters cleared up and lit the fire. I must go. This must be followed up immediately, before he can bolt abroad. Thank you, Mrs Cunningham. Thank you very much.' The Detective Inspector's voice was steeped in sincerity. He jumped to his feet. 'We'd have got there in the end, but you've been an enormous help. How much was the coffee?'

'Have it on me,' I said.

He nodded and hurried out of the lounge. There was a fresh spring in his step.

'You men are all so impetuous,' Beth said peevishly. 'I hadn't finished, not by a mile. And if he thinks that he's going to find Mr Macevoy lurking under the floorboards he's got another think coming.'

'How do you make that out?' I asked her. 'I thought that that was exactly what you were predicting.'

'Think about it a little more,' Beth said. 'For years, Mrs Macevoy's been living in that house in some style, paying her taxes, running a swish car and going for cruises. I don't see any scandal-rag paying so much for "My Life With A Sex Fiend" that it would support that kind of lifestyle indefinitely.'

'She seems to have been pally with Sir Ian,' Henry suggested. 'He may have been keeping her.'

'That man wouldn't keep her in tampons,' Beth snapped.

I was struggling to catch up. 'You think that she was sharing the hoard with the nephew?'

'She's hardly the type to let him collar the lot. And then, can you see Mr Macevoy arriving home, finding that the nest-egg that I suppose he was counting on to take him abroad had been frittered away by his two nearest relatives and then killing one of them and settling down happily with the other one – the one who shopped him years before?'

'Now that you mention it,' I said thoughtfully, 'no.'

'She didn't seem to have any lumps on her,' Henry said reflectively. 'Nor did she have the air of one who is acting under duress.'

'Well now,' said Beth, 'from what Daffy told us, Dougal was his nephew not hers. Dougal's mother was Mr Macevoy's sister.'

'Now you're losing me again,' I grumbled.

'Well, hang on to this. I don't know much about DNA and genetic fingerprints and all that stuff, but it does seem to me that if Dougal was Mr Macevoy's nephew they'd have enough bits of DNA in common to give the partial result that Inspector Ewell says the lab found.'

I had an uncomfortable feeling that Beth was going too fast. For one thing, Mr Macevoy would have needed to remain on the sweetest of terms with his wife if she was to give him food and shelter and not run to the police the first time that she went out to do the shopping. 'Let me see if I understand,' I said. 'You think that there was a fight and Dougal killed his uncle? And then decided to go into hiding? Why would he do that, rather than stay put and bluff it out?'

'You do want miracles, don't you?' Beth thought for about half a second. 'It seems to me that Mr Macevoy was the one with good reason to be angry. Or, at least, he would see it that way. My guess – and of course it is only a guess – is that there was a furious quarrel and he grabbed up the knife and Dougal got cut before he could get hold of it and stab his uncle. If a body turned up with a knife-blade or a stab-wound in it and Dougal was walking around with an obvious knife-slash, somebody would make the connection. So Dougal decided to vanish. If they managed to get rid of the body successfully, he could always surface again with a story about an accident and loss of memory, which would explain both the scar and his disappearance. Maybe he intended to do that anyway after the cut had healed.'

'And you think,' said Henry, 'that Inspector Ewell will surround the place with cries of, "Come out of there, Mr Macevoy, with your hands up," and out will come Dougal Webb?'

'Now you're making it sound silly. But yes. And if you still think I'm wrong, think about this. Mrs Macevoy was buying courgettes and pork chops. You know how Dougal drooled at the thought of either of those foods. And now,' Beth said, 'we must move. There are dogs to walk and a ravenous mouth to feed—'

'You mean Sam?' I asked.

'Who else? A ravenous mouth to feed and Isobel will be wondering if she's lost a husband.'

'My goodness, yes!' said Henry.

Chapter Ten

Whatever might be the outcome of Detective Inspector Ewell's activities, we could be assured of a visit from the police within the next day or two. We waited through the next day, but the only tidings to filter through to us came from a neighbour who had been told that somebody else had caught a mention on local radio of the arrest of some unspecified person on an unspecified charge

The expected visit came on the afternoon of the following day. What was unexpected was that this time DS Bremner was not dancing attendance on DI Ewell but on Detective Superintendent Aicheson. The Superintendent was a stout man. His colour was high, his ears and nose almost scarlet. I guessed that there was a race on between retirement and a coronary. And they wished to interview Beth and Hannah and me, one at a time. Daffy was away in my car, fetching a supply of feed from a new source and some of the dried ewes' milk which we swear by for pregnant bitches, nursing mothers and puppies. Henry had gone down with Isobel's 'flu and Isobel was at home attending to him. Our resources were seriously stretched.

I jumped to the conclusion that their mission was concerned with Beth's advice to Mr Ewell. 'Do you really need me as well as Mrs Cunningham?' I asked peevishly. 'I was just going to take a couple of dogs to the Moss.'

'We'll see you first,' said Mr Aicheson in tones which suggested that he was doing me a great favour.

Before I had time to think, I was whisked into my own sitting room. I met Beth's startled eyes over the Sergeant's shoulder and then the door closed between us.

When I had met Superintendent Aicheson on a previous occasion I had gained the impression that he was the political and administrative guru rather than an involved member of the crime detection teams. It was soon clear that he was present mainly to lend authority to the Sergeant. Most of the questions were hers.

Her line of questioning took me by surprise. She was brisk and businesslike and her manner was hostile. Evidently she was not yet willing to forgive and forget the incident in the farmyard involving her car. Instead of concentrating on the events leading up to our meeting with DI Ewell, she took me back to the evening of Dougal Webb's disappearance. Had Beth and I been together for the whole evening? What corroborating details could I remember? I told her that we had watched the video of a film, hired in Cupar. What film? I had to outline the plot for her. Unfortu-

nately, the film had proved a disappointment and my
memory of it was patchy.

She switched to the subject of Hannah. What did
we really know of her movements that night? How
could we be sure that her phone call had come from
Ardrossie? Did she have access to Henry's mobile
phone, or any other? Had the sound of the connection
been consistent with a public call-box? The questions
seemed to follow a path of logic which was unmistakable yet not on my mental map. I gave up trying to
orient myself and concentrated on recalling the truth.
We were innocent and therefore had nothing to fear,
that was my simple philosophy, and I hoped that Beth
would be wise enough to follow it.

We came back to the attempted blackmail. How
had I really felt about Dougal Webb prior to that
attempt? What grounds had I had for thinking him
untrustworthy? I had rejected his first approach, that
much was confirmed by the barmaid, but if he had
not vanished, if he had come back with more specific
threats, would I not have sacrificed my Dickson rather
than have him approach the Kennel Club?

At that point I got a little heated. When the
Sergeant uttered the word 'gun', her tone made it clear
that she considered my Dickson to be a trivial but
antisocial toy. I explained in forceful terms that, firstly,
there was no substance in Webb's allegations and, sec-
ondly, that the chance to acquire a Dickson Round
Action in mint condition comes but once in a lifetime
to a man of limited means and it would have taken
considerably more than Dougal Webb's threats to part

me from it. Even as I spoke I realized that I must be giving the impression that I would have killed to keep the gun, but I was still relying on truth and justice. Others have done the same and lived to regret it.

The Sergeant brought us round to the story of Mim. Surely there must have been conspiracy with Quentin Cove? How else could he have hoped to get away with such a fraud? Had money changed hands? Or favours? Had the quarrel in the farmyard occurred because I was trying to deny my part in the conspiracy and leave Mr Cove to face the music alone? I pointed out that I had signed Mim's registration over to Daffy long before Quentin Cove expressed any interest in the little bitch, but the Sergeant waved that aside as a palpable smoke-screen.

Part of my mind could see where the questions were leading while the rest of it was refusing to see anything of the sort. But one thing both parts of my mind were agreed on. No detective sergeant, even one as alluring as Detective Sergeant Bremner and supported by no less than a detective superintendent, was going to badger me with untrue and unsupported allegations. 'I have one question of my own,' I said. 'Who or what did Detective Inspector Ewell find yes-terday?'

The Sergeant tilted her head back in order to look down her nose at me. 'You'll know soon enough,' she said ominously. 'For now, we'll ask the questions.'

I had had enough. I explained clearly and almost politely that, failing any questions which did not pre-suppose that I was guilty of something, I would only be prepared to continue in the presence of my solicitor. Beth, I said, could make up her own mind and usually did. And with that I made what I hoped was a dignified exit, no doubt leaving the two officers with the worst possible impression.

Beth was somewhere upstairs. I could hear her clattering around angrily. Hannah, with Sam's help, was washing puppy dishes in the kitchen but the Sergeant steered me past and I had the feeling of being watched until I had left the gate with two of the dogs.

The weather gods had relented and given us one of those days that delude us into thinking that winter in Scotland isn't so bad after all. Even the Moss was not quite as barren as usual. The dogs were enjoying it as much as I was and they wanted to romp, so I kept my mind on controlling them and saw no reason to hurry back.

We returned to Three Oaks as dusk was falling, pleasantly tired and with three wood pigeon in the bag, taken on the flight-line to the pond for their evening's drink before going to roost. Both dogs had pleased me by retrieving the pigeon – the loose-feathered birds are not to every dog's taste. Quentin Cove's car was parked beside the police Range Rover in front of the house but the man himself was waiting at the gate. My interlude of escape was over and reality came pouring in.

'I must speak to you,' he said. 'Whatever you think of me, it's high time that we compared notes.'

'Hold on a minute longer,' I told him. Hannah came out of the house to meet me. The dogs were wet and smelly but she took them over without demur while avoiding any glance in the direction of the farmer.

I turned back. He met me beside his car. 'You've got a bloody nerve,' I said.

He looked shamefaced and I noticed that he seemed to have lost weight, but he managed a shrug. 'All right, so I've sinned. And I'm regretting it, every moment. I thought I could get away with it. Then I thought that I could live with it. But I can't.'

He had surprised and partially disarmed me by not being defiant, but I had no intention of allowing him to emulate the Prodigal Son. 'I'm not talking about the fiddle. But Daffy,' I said. 'You failed to get her banned from driving so you drove your car at her.'

He rubbed a hand over his face. 'I must have been horn daft. But – can you understand this? Something grand was disintegrating in my hands. I'll make it up to Mrs Mearns if ever I can.' The evening was cooling fast. He saw me shiver and remorse turned to compassion. 'Come into the car,' he said. We got in and he started the engine and turned up the heat. He sat looking out of the windscreen at nothing for a long moment. 'I've had it easy for most of my life,' he said. 'Hard physical work, but you can take that if your health's good and you've got security. My granddad was a thrifty farmer. He bought Ardrossie outright and worked it up. My dad added to it. It came to me as a going concern at a time when a farmer couldn't lose money if he tried. I never faced a challenge, never achieved anything on my own.'

I was damned if I was going to feel sorry for him. 'There was the dog-food,' I said.

He shook his head. He was not to be coaxed out of his self-pity. Poor little rich boy, I thought. 'That was no challenge. It was as if the set-up was there already, waiting to happen. The right men gave me the right advice and it worked. But all my life I've had dogs. I might've gone in for sheepdog trialling, but Ardrossie's never been a sheep farm and gun dogs are the dogs I know. You heard of the man who said, "I'd give my right arm to be ambidextrous"?'

'I have now.'

'Well, that's how I felt. It was over the top, I can see that now. From here on, if I hear the word "obsession" I'll ken just what it means. But I found myself with a dog that could win. I've had some good dogs in the past, but aye with some fault – sometimes an inherent fault but often because, when I was young and inexperienced, I tried to hurry the dog along too quickly. But this time the bitch and I were in tune. You know what I mean?'

'Of course I do,' I said. I had experienced that supreme harmony perhaps a dozen times and lesser likenesses of it with two dogs out of three.

He sighed. 'Just for once, I could have gone in and matched myself against you and all the others. It drove me frantic that I couldn't run my wee bitch because of some rule that you said was nonsense and even I could see was doing nothing but prevent improvement of the working breeds. For a while, that was all I could think of. When I came to my senses, I gave thanks that I hadn't done more damage than I have. But I didn't want to do Mrs Mearns any real harm. And I didn't mean to land you in it.'

I felt a prickling of my scalp. 'Have you landed me – us – in it?'

'I hope no, but I'm feared I have. Yon Inspector Ewell arrived this afternoon with a sergeant mannie I'd not seen before. He was polite as ever, the Inspector, but under the politeness he was rock-hard. He wouldn't tell me a damn thing—'

'I know the feeling,' I said.

'—but, reading between the lines, they've decided that no one person did the deed.'

'But which deed?' I asked. 'I might be able and willing to help them if I knew what the crime was.'

'Do you not know? I found out that much – no thanks to Mr Detective Inspector Ewell,' he added bitterly. 'I had it from Elsie Dundee. They went to Gifford House yesterday and found Mr Macevoy in a hidey-hole under the floor. She saw them taking him away. So it seems that the body must have been Dougal's.'

So Beth had been wrong for once. I must remember to crow over her. 'Then what's all this fuss about?' I asked. 'If Mr Macevoy killed his nephew . . .'

'But he didn't. They seem quite sure of that, I don't know why.' The light was almost gone. Quentin Cove's voice was coming out of darkness but he sounded both plaintive and indignant. 'They seem to have eliminated every individual – so far as they know of them – with any reason to resent Dougal. Likely they're looking for other blackmail victims. But they've also decided that more than one person must have been involved.'

I thought that over, liking it less and less. The field was wide open again.

'It's a bugger,' he resumed suddenly. 'They must have decided that either I killed him over the blackmail or your Miss Hopewell stabbed him in a fit of jealous rage. The fact that I have a rock-solid alibi up to the wee small hours seems to strike them as the most suspicious factor of all. Even if young Hannah was guilty, she could never have moved the body to Gifford Hill on her own. She'd have had to have help.'

For a moment I considered myself as a suspect. Apart from the fact that I knew myself to be innocent, it made a tenable theory. 'Goddamn!' I said.

'Takes a wheen of getting used to, doesn't it?'

I let that pass as irrelevant. 'Do you know whether they've found where he was killed? Or where the knife came from? Or where the handle ended up?'

'It doesn't seem like it. I left them rummaging around the farm. I'll tell you this – if I come across a knife-handle around the place, it goes in the bottom of the midden. That's the one place they've shied away from. And they kept me away from the phone, so I decided the damage was done and I might just as well come here.'

'They'll have seen us comparing notes,' I pointed out.

'Guilty or innocent, they'd expect that.'

We fell silent again. My mouth had dried and I could feel tension in my stomach and in my neck muscles. Bad events were in the wind. My mind wanted to rush off in all directions but I held it, by effort of will, to a pattern of logic.

Could Hannah be guilty? It was physically possible. Would she kill a faithless lover? Unlikely. I would have expected her reaction to be hysteria rather than violence, but who knew the reaction of a woman scorned? Would Quentin Cove have helped her to dispose of a body? Very unlikely – unless, of course, she had inherited his secret from Dougal or deduced it for herself. She might have threatened to incriminate him with the murder. If they had been acting in concert . . . Immediately, the conundrum began to resemble the old riddle about two brothers, one of whom always tells lies while the other tells the truth. You have one question to determine which is which. The answer to the riddle, of course, is to ask one of them, 'What would your brother answer, if I asked him whether he was the liar?' Except that on this merry-go-round there was no brother who could be trusted to tell the truth.

But again, Hannah had never been a competent liar. Her few attempts at pulling the wool over our eyes had been accompanied by so much blushing, hesitation, finger-twisting and contradiction as to be wholly transparent. As I remembered her voice on the phone and her behaviour the next morning, each had been more in accordance with puzzlement than with a terrible secret.

Quentin Cove, now, was speaking from the standpoint of one who is innocent; but then, what else would he do? His story was confirmed by his friends and then by Hannah . . . up to around four in the morning. By then, time would be short. Dawn would still be several hours away but it had been a clear night and I recalled a rising moon. The sky had still been clear in the morning. In the country, even in winter, people are up and about early. Postmen, milkmen, lorry drivers, wildfowlers and others would have been on the roads. Elsie Dundee lived nearby. Easy enough, perhaps, to stop a vehicle for a few seconds and tuck the body away behind the hedge, to walk back after hiding the vehicle . . . but I could not visualize any murderer daring to carry a body up a hill that was overlooked by a road and several houses, except perhaps in the dead hours just after midnight or after waiting for an overcast night. Even then, the task would be impossible without torches which might attract the attention of passers-by.

Suppose that Cove had killed Dougal Webb before leaving home, or that there had been another confrontation over the attempted blackmail when Webb returned home, after Hannah gave up and left. The factory would have been standing empty. I had been shown round it by the proud farmer. Most of the raw materials went up by conveyor into the silos and from there to top of the square tower. Nearly all the processing took place in the tower as the product progressed downwards under gravity, untouched by hand and usually unseen by eye. The ground floor was given over mainly to storage and packing, and most of the human activity was on this level. A body, wrapped in polythene, could be hidden in the tower for a day or two in safety, especially if the proprietor was on hand to allocate duties. The polythene could then be used to wrap a large order, thus to disappear for ever.

Also on the ground floor was an area given over to the preparation of animal products, in machinery derived from the fast-food industry. Originally, Quentin Cove had bought his animal products already prepared but later he had decided that he was being ripped off. Dog feeds are subject to scrutiny at least as stringent as that given to human food, and sudden trouble with the inspectorate had been the last straw. Cove had struck a deal with a large concern specializing in poultry for the human market, to buy their leftovers. To these were added a steady stream of rabbit meat. At first glance, an hour spent feeding the parts of a body through those machines would have seemed a safer means of disposal than moving it to the bonfire on Gifford Hill. But the police had not missed the point. They had checked for human tissue and Cove might well have anticipated their action. He was not a fool.

'What did Inspector Ewell want to know?' I asked.

I felt Quentin Cove jump and thought that he might have been on the point of falling asleep. Stress often has that effect. The car was becoming hot. He turned the fan down. 'Nothing very much,' he said. 'What I was doing every bloody minute since I reached puberty and who could bear me out. How I got on with you and those girls of yours. And then he was wanting to know about the blackmail.'

'You didn't give in to young Webb, did you?' I asked.

He grunted in annoyance. 'It was all very well for you,' he said. 'Dougal was barking up the wrong tree. You really kenned damn-all about it. But he had me by the short and curlies and he knew it fine. He could get my trialling stopped dead before it had hardly started. But he was dashed queer about it,' Quentin added. 'It was as if he didn't expect it to make a difference between us. He seemed to think that things could go on just as before.'

'Just like you do, in fact,' I said.

'Nah,' he said glumly after a moment's thought. 'I don't think anything like that. I've made an idiot of myself and I know it.'

I decided to dangle a little bait. 'What did he want from you? Money?'

'I don't know that he ever asked anyone for money. No, when he came to the point it was little enough. He wanted my video recorder. It was a good one, mind, top of the range, but it had been playing me up now and again and I'd been looking at a newer model. Living on my own, I like having a quality video machine and watching the things I want to see when I want to see them, not when some clown of a pro- grammer thinks it's time I sat down. But I wouldn't kill to keep it, even if I couldn't have afforded another dozen of the things.'

It certainly seemed an inadequate motive for murder – if true. But there is no way to predict what a man will do in a sudden fit of rage. Quentin Cove had never been one to go around looking for a fight, but he had a temper . . .

I was wondering how to probe a little further without testing that temper too far, when the static scene began to shift. The outside light sprang to life. Sergeant Bremner and Superintendent Aicheson came out of the house. They got into the Range Rover and the Sergeant drove off without, apparently, even a glance in our direction.

The Range Rover was hardly out of the drive before the door opened again and Beth emerged, wrapped in a tartan shawl. We got out of the car to meet her but she hopped up into the back seat of the big car. 'We have to talk,' she told the farmer, 'but you are not crossing my threshold again.'

I heard the farmer make a small sound. I had heard him make the same sound when he caught his finger in a gate.

We got back into the front. While the courtesy light was still on I saw that Quentin Cove had flushed dark red and his square face looked haggard. 'I was just telling John how much I regret—'

'No time for that now,' Beth snapped. 'Tell Daffy all about it later. She may forgive you. I certainly wouldn't. I saw you out here ages ago, John, but I wasn't going to let Sam join in with us so I had to wait until they'd finished with Hannah. She came out of there in tears, so she and Sam can look after each other for a while.'

'They found Mr Macevoy at Gifford House,' I told her. 'But they've cleared him of the murder somehow.'

'I got that much out of them. They told me about it, just to shut me up. They've found the lorry driver who gave him a lift from York to Kirkcaldy on the Monday, the day after Dougal disappeared.'

I began to repeat our discussion but Beth cut me off. She was in her overdrive. 'All right. So I was wrong. You can crow about it later. They've made up their minds that there had to be a conspiracy. They're probably right. Dougal was no lightweight. I don't see any one man carrying him up that hill and over that sort of ground single-handed. And in their minds a conspiracy means us.'

'There's one other possibility,' Quentin Cove said. 'Jim Macevoy could have reached home and found his wife wondering what to do with the body of his nephew.'

'Do you think she'd be much help, carrying a body across that broken ground by night?' Beth asked.

'At least it wouldn't be uphill,' Cove pointed out.

'The police wouldn't have missed that option,' I said, 'but they seem to have discounted it. We never met Macevoy. How old was he when he went inside?'

'In his fifties.'

'He must be sixty or more by now,' Beth said. 'Could you picture him managing the body with no help except for his wife? She looked like a flabby lump to me, the one time I saw her.'

'You're right,' Cove said gloomily.

'I may not be. People can perform amazing feats

when they're desperate. But we can't bank on it. Our problem,' Beth said firmly, 'is that while the police are looking at us they may not be looking at anybody else. They can't bring a case against any of us because there isn't any real evidence and there never will be. The fiscal hasn't yet called for an inquiry in front of the sheriff, but when it happens the facts will come out. And we'll be smeared, for ever. Not openly but by implication. If they don't make an arrest, we'll have this around our necks for years. Hannah, in particular, may go down in folklore as the girl who got away with murdering her lover. We've got to do something.'

'Definitely,' I said. 'But what?'

Beth thought it over for all of ten seconds. 'We only have long shots,' she said, 'so we'd better . . . what does one do with long shots?'

'Back them,' Cove said.

'Right. Mr Cove, can you get us into Dougal's cottage? Or have the police sealed it?'

'No problem. But you're probably too late. The seals have been broken. Somebody went through the place – probably more than one person. The police know, but they haven't bothered to seal it again. I took a look inside for myself. Nothing seems to have been stolen, so I jalouse it was somebody looking for whatever Dougal had been holding over them.'

'They probably found it,' I said. 'It's hopeless, isn't it? If somebody already got screwed for a car or a watch – or a video – his motive's gone. He never seems to have bitten the same person twice.'

'Thanks very much,' Cove said.

Beth leaned forward. 'But we don't know that,' she said. 'Mr Cove, what was the next demand he made on you? What was the next guilty secret? Did he find some trace of Daffy on the bull-bars at the front of this car? Was he going to turn you in for attempted murder?'

'Nothing of the sort!' Quentin Cove's voice went up through the roof. I could sense his outrage. It was as unmistakable as a fart in the confined space. 'I'd been daft for a while, I admit it. I did three things I'll be bitterly ashamed of for the rest of my days.'

'Four,' I said. 'You let my tyres down.'

'All right, four. Dougal spotted the switch of dogs and he took my video off me and that's all. Damn it, Dougal was already dead when . . . when I . . .'

'When you tried to injure Daffy. All right,' Beth said. 'Keep your socks on. I wanted to be sure. Who else is there? Mr Cove, you were closer to him, geographically, than anyone else. What expensive toys did he have? The car, the watch, the video. What else?'

'Clothes,' I said.

'You can't blackmail somebody for clothes,' Beth snapped. 'At least you could, but there's nobody I can think of whose clothes would have fitted Dougal. What else did he covet?'

'I've no idea,' Cove said. 'We didn't let our hair down and have heart-to-heart blethers.'

'I must ask Hannah,' Beth said musingly. 'Yes, I think we definitely want a look inside his cottage.'

'Whatever you're after, it's probably gone,' I told her. 'The victim took it back. Or the police have it. We might get a solicitor to ask for disclosure of what they've found.'

'Later,' Beth said. 'First, let's be sure that it's gone. You'll be at home in the morning?'

'I'll watch for you,' said Quentin Cove.

'Right,' Beth said. 'And until then, you bastard, behave yourself, you hear me?' As she got out of the car and the courtesy light came on, her elbow gave him an accidental crack over the head that made his eyes water.

Chapter Eleven

I was in no doubt that Beth's view of our predicament was the right one. We had seen other instances in which the law and justice had failed to coincide. A verdict of *not guilty* was often taken to mean *got away with it*. *Not proven* was worse. And if no charge was brought against anybody, that could be the worst of all because there would not even be the cold comfort of either of the other verdicts. The odium would stick. Hannah would be tainted for ever and – God help us! – the whisper might go round that she and I had conspired to kill her lover in order to further an affair of our own. Such a rumour would be no more unreasonable than many that had circulated on the local gossip-vine.

When I mentioned the danger to Beth, she only nodded. I realized then that she was, as so often, ahead of me and that this had been one of the reasons for her call to arms. My ambition to drop Sir Ian Bewlay into the mire up to and over his balding head would have to take second place for the moment.

I was in a fever to dash around and do something, anything, to upset the *status quo*, but Beth calmed me down and set me to clearing the decks for the morning. I spent the rest of the day walking dogs in the darkness and helping with the last feed and clean. Beth, meanwhile, was in her hyperactive mode, pulling more than her weight around the kennels, comforting Hannah until Daffy's return relieved her of that necessity, attending to Sam and between times making phone call after phone call. And somehow during all this frenzy a meal made it onto the table.

Sam, protesting loudly that he wanted to see his favourite video for the thousandth time, was soon banished to bed and we settled in the kitchen with Hannah and Daffy – not in order to enjoy our knocking-off drinks, long after our usual time, but to take them anyway as a comfort and a lubricant to serious discussion.

Hannah was still red-eyed and bemused by being pitched suddenly into a strange new world, but when Beth pressed her for details of what Detective Sergeant Bremner had asked her she pulled herself together. She told us that the Sergeant, after the now customary minute-by-minute dissection of Hannah's activities over what seemed to be an unnecessarily prolonged period, had suddenly changed tack. Had Hannah quarrelled with Dougal? Had she been jealous? Or had he tried to blackmail her? Into sleeping with him, perhaps? What threat had he held over her? 'And then,' Hannah said indignantly, 'she up and asked me whether I fancied Mr Cunningham.'

'What did you tell her?' Daffy asked, enthralled.

'I told her that she had a mind like a cesspool and

that if she made any more suggestions like those I'd tell Mr Cunningham.'

The others laughed. I cringed. The idea that my wrath could constitute a threat to be held over the police was a new one to me, but it seemed that, rather than fancying me, Hannah still regarded me with awe. I was uncertain whether to be flattered or insulted.

Beth was trying, not very successfully, to hide a smile. 'What else?' she asked.

'Sergeant Bremner said that there were a carving knife and two smaller kitchen knives in Dougal's kitchen and she wanted to know if there should have been any other ones. I said that I didn't know. And was I sure that Mr Cunningham hadn't come to meet me that night? I said definitely not and anyway I had your car so he'd have had to walk about ten miles or take a taxi. Then she wanted to know if you'd ever seen that film before and I said that I knew for a fact that you hadn't. But she went on and on, suggesting things you'd hardly believe.'

'We'd believe them all right,' Beth said. 'But I'm afraid we may have to go on and on, like Sergeant Bremner. First . . . Daffy, Mrs Kitts may be back tomorrow if Mr Kitts is still improving. Either way, can you manage the place if Hannah comes with us tomorrow morning? We need to look through Dougal's cottage.'

'No problem,' said Daffy.

'But do you really need me?' Hannah asked nervously.

Beth paused for a moment, wondering whether

to be brisk or motherly and deciding to attempt a compromise. 'We do need you,' she said. 'It may be difficult for you and bring back all sorts of memories you'd rather put aside but you'll have to be brave. We have to untangle this horrible mess if you're not to be bothered again and again, so in a way it's for your own good. Mr Cove says that Dougal's cottage had been entered. You're the one person who may be able to give us a fresh lead by telling us whether anything's missing. Or if anything's there that wasn't there before. Or if there's anything there that he wouldn't have paid for but might have got by . . . by putting pressure on people.'

'By blackmail,' Hannah said stoutly. 'It's all right. I didn't know anything about it at the time and I didn't believe it at first, but thinking it over since then I've been remembering how he could set his heart on things. Not money, just things. And most of the time he did care about how people felt, but when he wanted something he changed completely and was ready to ride roughshod over anybody. I can easily believe that he'd use threats.'

Hannah had been pressed to accept a vodka and tonic instead of her usual shandy. Beth caught Daffy's eye and Daffy surreptitiously topped up Hannah's glass. The unaccustomed alcohol was having the desired effect of loosening her tongue, but what came out in response to Beth's probing was mostly negative. Did Dougal have any enemies? Not to say enemies but he didn't seem to get on with people. Then who were his friends? Hannah could only think of Elsie Dundee's son Jimmy, who on his visits home had usually gone for a pint with Dougal. Who else might he have been blackmailing? Hannah had no idea.

Beth sighed and held out her own glass for a refill. 'We have to get a starting point,' she said. 'And you're not being very helpful. Hannah, Dougal coveted things. Did he ever say, "I wish I had a such-and-such"?'

'Sometimes.' Hannah carefully suppressed a lady-like burp. 'In fact, quite often. It was his way. Mostly it was cars. He'd see a four-by-four, much more suitable for a farmer than the Lotus, and he'd say, "I could be doing with one of those." Once it was a real pearl necklace and he said, "I wish I could give you something like that," and I said that he didn't have to worry about it, I wasn't the sort to wear pearls, pearls would look silly on me.' Hannah blinked and hurried on. 'Sometimes, when we saw something happening, like an accident or a really weird car or once it was a girl with her skirt tucked into the back of her knickers, he'd say, "God, I wish I had a video camera!" And I remember him watching one of Mr Hatton's dogs working sheep and saying that about a camera and also saying, "I wish I owned that dog."'

'That's interesting,' Beth said. 'John, just suppose that he'd had something serious on you, something that you'd really hate for anyone to know, and he demanded that you hand over your favourite dog – which would that be?'

'I don't know,' I said. 'Probably Ash.'

'Well then, would you have killed him in order to keep the dog?'

I considered the question seriously. 'It would depend on circumstances,' I said. 'It's too easy to sit here and say "no". I'm not a killing sort of person except in the way of duty, but I'm no different from other men. If the demand came at the height of a furious quarrel I suppose it might prove to be the last straw.'

Beth looked at me speculatively and then decided on a change of subject. 'Hannah, can you think of anyone who'll be better off with Dougal dead?'

'I suppose his uncle . . .'

'Who was still hitch-hiking northward at the time. Did Dougal have any insurance policies?'

To my surprise, Hannah's glow was not just the firelight but a definite blush. 'That was another thing he said he wished he had. He said that he was going to start one for me. And once, when I admired his Lotus, he said that he was going to make out a will in my favour. But I don't know that he did either of those things.'

'Surely,' I said, 'if the police had found either a will or an insurance policy with you as the beneficiary, they'd have said something?'

'Well, I'm not sure,' Hannah said. 'Sergeant Bremner kept asking me things like what difference was Dougal's death going to make to me. I said that losing a boyfriend was bound to make a big change. Obviously. I wasn't going to give the impression that

I'd been expecting to be better off. But I think she knew.'

'Oh, my dear!' Beth said.

Isobel arrived on time in the morning. Henry, she said, was back on his feet, shaky but self-sufficient, and she was glad to get back to Three Oaks and less demanding patients. After a quick rush at the more demanding chores we were able to leave Three Oaks, confident that Daffy and Isobel could at least keep things ticking over. The morning was dank. We settled Sam in front of his favourite video, fobbed off Isobel's questions with a very brief résumé of events and made our escape.

At Ardrossie I turned into the farmyard. Quentin Cove was standing on the now exposed tarmac. He was talking to Detective Inspector Ewell.

'Oh, hell!' I said.

'I left a message for him,' Beth said firmly, 'asking him to meet us here. But I didn't think that he'd come. I just wanted to be able to show, afterwards, that we hadn't done anything behind his back.'

'He won't want us sifting through Dougal's home.'

'We'll see,' Beth retorted.

I drew up beside the two-year-old Allegro which I assumed had brought the Inspector. He seemed to be unaccompanied. 'He's become the enemy,' I said.

'I don't think so. But that's why I didn't tell you sooner,' she said obscurely.

We disembarked. Ewell walked to meet us while

Quentin Cove kept his distance and looked ready to take to his heels. I could guess that Ewell had not been offering words of comfort.

'If you've abandoned us to the wolves . . .' I began.

Ewell shook his head sadly. 'None of my doing,' he said. 'I suspect that the Super gained the impression from Sergeant Bremner that I was going easy on you.' He saw my eyebrows go up. I was always a believer in loyalty to my immediate superior. 'I'm not blaming the lassie,' he added quickly. 'She wouldn't run with tales. But if the Super asked her a direct question, she'd have to give an honest opinion.'

'Maybe,' I said. I had a suspicion that the knives might be out for Detective Inspector Ewell, who was too unsophisticated a man to realize it. What I was much more certain of was that Ewell was not above moderating his own opinions for the sake of a pretty face; but I had already known that from his fatherly attitude to Beth over the years.

Ewell ignored the doubt in my voice and nodded. 'They're checking over the possibilities of conspiracy while I'm relegated to searching for the murder scene. If we find that, we'll have the case cracked, I'm thinking. If not, then it may hang over us for years.'

'You don't have a lot to go on,' I agreed.

'We've nothing,' he said disgustedly. 'A body largely cremated. Its immediate vicinity also burned. A knife-blade that could have come from anywhere. A victim who has been practising extortion by menaces, which means that damn near anyone might have a motive for killing him, but who's to know? And to cap it all, men and dogs were scampering round and around the body,' Ewell said bitterly, 'before we got there and even afterwards. Not a footprint to be found that didn't belong to one of you men or Mrs Dundee or the foresters or your damn dogs. Or the rabbits, of course.'

'They surely can't blame you for that,' said Beth. 'The night's rain would have washed any older footprints away.'

Anyone but Beth would have received a sharp retort. 'I'd like to think so,' the Detective Inspector told her. 'But when your message said that you could give us a fresh lead . . .'

'I only said that I hoped that I could make a contribution,' Beth said. 'Mr Aicheson won't find the truth by looking at us. And that's all we want, the same as yourself – the truth. And we have a right to make our own investigation in order to establish our innocence, don't we?'

'As early as this, I doubt it,' Ewell said. 'It may depend what you had in mind.'

Beth smiled at him winningly. 'Nothing outrageous. But it's our only starting-point. You'll have searched Mr Webb's cottage up, down and sideways. But would you have known if something had been removed or shifted or put back? Or even added? You didn't ask Hannah, and she'd be more likely to know than anyone.'

'Well, it's a thought,' Ewell said doubtfully

'So I phoned you. The seals are already broken. If Hannah says that something isn't where it belongs, you can tell us whether the police took it or moved it.

And if we find something useful, we'd rather find it in your presence. Otherwise somebody could say that we'd put it there.'

Ewell raised a tired eyebrow. 'They could say that anyway. As you remind me, the seals were broken.'

'We'll worry about that if it happens,' Beth said firmly. 'First, let's try to find something, if it's there to be found.' As she led the way imperiously to the cottage door she beckoned to Quentin Cove, who followed obediently in her train, producing a large old-fashioned key. The door opened directly into a compact living room.

At first glance the cottage seemed to have been the habitation of an untidy man leading a slovenly, bachelor existence; but I heard Hannah draw in breath in a disapproving hiss and when I looked again I could see an underlying orderliness. I realized then that a police search followed by any number of more amateurish searches could have disarranged even the British Museum. If everything was not in its place, at least there was a place for everything. Cupboards and shelves had been made or adapted by a loving hand to suit the intended contents which had now been replaced higgledy-piggledy or dropped on the floor.

Inspector Ewell had been carrying a large envelope. 'I was coming here anyway, one of these days,' he said. 'We took away his video cassettes for study.' He produced four cassettes and set them on a shelf which had evidently been made for them under the video recorder. There was room for many more. It seemed that Dougal Webb had intended to tape whatever took his fancy.

'Did they hold any interest?' I asked the Inspector.

He grunted and shook his head. 'They didn't interest me. Sitcoms, and I'd seen most of them.'

Beth decided to begin at the top and work down. The small cottage would only have had one small bedroom and possibly a boxroom tucked under the slates. Beth, Inspector Ewell and Hannah would have filled the available space. I could hear Hannah protesting that she had never seen Dougal's bedroom but to no avail. Quentin Cove stayed with me.

Most of the furnishings were utilitarian and slightly shabby, as befitted a young and newly qualified farm manager, but one exception stood out. I drew Quentin Cove's attention to a small but handsome Victorian dining table which took up more than its share of the limited floor-space. I stroked its deep gloss and it seemed to purr. 'This is a bit up-market compared to the rest,' I said. 'The product of blackmail? Or was there a legacy?'

Cove shook his head. 'The product of a roup. We were at a farm sale together. I bought some calves and he paid about a fiver for the table. It was in a barn, covered with chicken-shit. It took him a month of evenings and weekends to clean it up and restore the finish.'

So another promising lead was a dead end. I decided that if the table came to Hannah I would make her an offer for it. The cottage was very cold. The electric heating had been turned off by some frugal busybody. Even through my favourite sheepskin coat I was becoming chilled. Between that and the nervous tension, I was soon in dire need of a pee.

I could have stepped outside but I would have been under the windows of the house or the cottage, possibly both. 'Is the bathroom working?' I asked the farmer.

He shook his head. 'Water's drained down in case of frost. Go over to the house. It's open and the water's on again.'

'Thanks.'

I hurried across to the house. I could hear voices. But Beth always insists on my drinking several mugs of tea with my breakfast in order to 'keep my fluids up', whatever that may mean, and I was in too much of a hurry to worry about visitors or even intruders in the farmhouse.

When I emerged some little while later Mrs Dundee, complete with pinny and duster, was in the hall together with a large young man in jeans and several heavy sweaters. He was bronzed and looked fit.

'It's Mr Cunningham, Jimmy,' she said delightedly. 'You can tell him. He'll ken fine what you should dae.'

The young man – Jimmy – shuffled his feet. 'I don't know, Ma,' he said.

'Weel,' said his mother, 'ye maun clype to some-body some time. Ye canna gang back tae your boat and leave us a wanrestfu. And it'll a be waur, gin they airt it oot an ye've no said.'

Ordinarily, I would have made an excuse and my

escape. But the farmhouse was warm while the world outside was not. I unbuttoned my coat, to let some more of the delicious warmth inside, and waited.

Evidently his mother's words were not only comprehensible but convincing to the young man. 'Maybe you're right,' he said at last. 'Mr Cunningham, can you spare a few minutes?'

I said that I could. But I had no intention of receiving his confidences while standing in a hallway which, for all its warmth, was distinctly draughty. I led the way into Quentin's sitting room, shed my heavy coat and got us comfortably seated.

It was a relief that Jimmy was a much clearer speaker than his mother. Dialects in Scotland change radically over comparatively short distances and my Edinburgh upbringing had not prepared me for Elsie Dundee. I had no doubt that when the two were alone he would go a long way towards matching his mother's unspoiled rural dialect, but school followed by work away from home had taught him the sort of English that passes muster anywhere. Looking at him, I could understand why there had been rumours about his parentage. I could see in him the image of a slimmer Sir Ian Bewlay but without a trace of the expressions of arrogance and guile.

'First,' he said, 'my mother tells me you were good to her while I was at sea. I want to pay you back and perhaps you'd square with Mr Kitts?'

He produced a healthy little roll of notes and pushed a Clydesdale tenner into my hand before falling silent. I guessed that he would be offended if I refused the money so I put it in my pocket, with the mental reservation that it would be available for Mrs Dundee if she should fall on hard times again.

'What did you want to tell me?' I prompted him.

He was silent for so long that I thought that he must have changed his mind, but eventually he stirred. 'The last time I was home, about two months ago, I was broke. I'd been cleaned out.'

'By a lassie. The leddies was aye taen up wi him,' his mother said proudly.

'Well, whatever,' said her son, avoiding my eye. 'I reached home in the afternoon. Mum wasn't in but I knew she'd be up at the Big House so I walked up there. Mrs Wartle, the housekeeper – she's the only steady staff Sir Ian keeps – she gave us a cup of tea in the kitchen. When she left the room with a tray, Mum asked if I had any money for her and I had to tell her that I was skint.

'I left soon after that and I walked along the front of the house, on the grass. As I came to a partly open window at the corner of the house I heard voices, and what they were saying stopped me as if I'd walked into a wall. "I'm sorry I made you show it to me now," Sir Ian's voice said. "And I certainly wouldn't want anyone else to see it. I hope you were damn careful with the editing." And another man asked him what he thought – just being sarcastic, you understand? And Sir Ian said that he'd better chuck the master tape away, and the unedited copy, because they could be worth money in the wrong quarter.

'I managed a peep in at the window without being

seen. The two of them were watching the TV screen. The other man was that wee feller that hangs around with Sir Ian.'

'Timothy Pratt?' I suggested.

'That's the one. Just then there was a knock on the door and Sir Ian switched off the video and the telly damn quick. It was Mrs Wartle, telling them that their afternoon tea was set in the drawing room. She stood holding the door, so they upped and went, leaving things as they were.

'Well, Mr Cunningham, I'm not a dishonest man. But it seemed to me that Sir Ian had been taking advantage of my mother for years and not paying her a proper wage. And I was needing a wee bit of cash to leave with her. So I pushed up the window and hopped over the sill. They had to have been talking about the video. I ejected the cassette – we have one on the ship, so I knew how to work it. Sir Ian had a whole shelf of cassettes, some of them unused, so I put one of those in the video recorder instead and put the real one in my pocket and slid back out of the window and pulled it down after me. My heart was knocking so's I thought they'd hear it in the drawing room.

'I was away back to the road before I thought how I was going to get my hands on any of the money Sir Ian had talked about.

'It would be some little while before Ma got home. The other person I always saw on my leaves was Dougal Webb, so I walked to Ardrossie. Dougal was ready to finish for the day, and he took me in and gave me a dram.'

Jimmy Dundee paused in his tale and looked me in the eye. 'They tell me that Dougal was going in for a bit of blackmail. I can't say I'm as surprised as I might have been. I'd thought about borrowing some money from him to give to Ma, but I put that out of my mind. He could be good company, but when it came to money he was hard as stone. And he was impatient. He was ready to work for what he wanted, but he wanted a hell of a lot and he expected it to drop into his lap straight away instead of after years of sweat. But I never knew that he was a wrong 'un. I thought that he was just clever at driving a deal. That's how he explained away his car to me and he seemed to believe it himself.'

'I think he probably did,' I said.

'Likely. He certainly had me convinced. And he seemed just the sort to give me the advice I was needing. So I told him the story and he said to leave the tape with him and he'd take a look at it.

'I saw him again just before I went back to sea. He slipped me fifteen quid and told me that he was going to give Sir Ian a fright. He wouldn't say what was on the tape. I left it at that and off I went, but first I made him promise to do nothing for a while, so's nobody could guess that it was me that took it.' Jimmy looked at me anxiously. 'Mr Cunningham, I'm in no hurry to go and tell the police that I nicked something out of Marksmuir House. But Dougal's been killed and if this has any relevance they'll have to know. Right?'

'Absolutely right,' I said. All of a sudden my head, from being a vessel filled only with despondency, was

buzzing with ideas. 'Leave it with me. I'll keep you out
of it if I can.'

'There now!' said Mrs Dundee.

I hurried back across the yard. Was it too much to
hope that the compromising video cassette was still
around? That it had been missed by the police and by
other searchers? Probably, yes, much too much. But
at least we had the possible starting-point that we had
lacked.

The whole party was again crammed into the small
sitting room. Hannah looked at me as I entered. 'His
new jacket's missing,' she said sadly. 'So he did mean
to come and meet me.' She seemed to take some
comfort from the thought that her lover had not deliberately stood her up.

Beth resumed questioning a now peevish Hannah
about the source of every object of any value, about
most of which Hannah had not the least idea. I drew
Detective Inspector Ewell aside. 'Are you sure that
there was nothing missed on those video tapes?'

'Positive. I watched them myself, every inch, even
the blank bits.'

I approached the video recorder, studied the
switches for a moment and turned it on. There was
no little symbol to indicate that a cassette was in place
but I pressed the Eject button anyway. Nothing happened. My new-found optimism sagged. The
compromising cassette had either been recovered or
it was too well hidden even for a police search.

'Try it again,' said Quentin Cove. 'There's a fault.
That's why I didn't mind parting with it. The little

symbol doesn't light and it usually takes three or four tries before it'll eject.'

'You never mentioned that to our officers,' Ewell said bitterly.

'They wouldn't let me be present during the search,' said Quentin Cove.

I tried the rewind button and got leftward arrow symbols and a whirring sound. I switched on the television set and picked up the remote control. Usually the highest numbered channel is tuned to a video recorder. As the tape clunked to a halt, I tried Channel 9 and pressed 'Play' on the machine. A series of images flashed and vanished. Then the screen steadied. There was no soundtrack.

The others gathered round.

We were looking through the windscreen of a car just coming to a halt. Then the camera was carried out of the car and set down carefully on the bonnet, looking ahead. It showed a motorbike, damaged and lying on its side in the road, close beside a stone wall. The rider, still helmeted, lay pinned beneath it. He seemed to be unconscious. From the marks on the verge and the positions of bike and rider it seemed that the rider had lost control and slammed at speed into the wall.

The picture moved slightly as another person got out of the car. Then into the frame came Sir Ian Bewlay and Timothy Pratt. Sir Ian was already speaking into his mobile phone.

The two men examined the unconscious rider and gently felt his limbs for fractures. Their faces were always in sight and I had no doubt that a show was being put on for the camera. Sir Ian took off his coat and spread it over the rider. Pratt, in his turn, folded his own coat and slipped it under the man's head. He checked that the man's tongue was forward. They stood back, satisfied. Pratt glanced at his watch.

Sir Ian took out a cigar, lit it and dropped the match.

The motorbike must have been spilling its fuel. Immediately, the rider was enveloped in a spectacular ball of flames.

Sir Ian jumped back, out of the frame, and was not seen again.

To do him justice, Pratt did what he could. The flames were rising as more fuel leaked from the motorbike. Pratt grabbed the man by his clothing and pulled him away from the pool of burning fuel, but the man's leathers must have been soaked with the petrol. Pratt ran out of the picture. He returned in a few seconds carrying a rug with which he tried to smother the flames that still enveloped the man. This was the sequence that had appeared on television and attracted to Pratt such favourable publicity. The film ran on until the arrival of the ambulance and the fire brigade. By then, I was in no doubt that the man was as good as dead. Pratt, who had himself been burned, had behaved with courage; but he would undoubtedly be damned when it was known that he had suppressed the part of the film showing the origin of the fire.

The sequence gave way to a dark frame with white speckles, indicating no signal.

There was absolute silence except for the faintest whisper from the machinery. Nobody wanted to be the first to speak. I stopped the machine. At the third try, it ejected the tape. I handed it to the Detective Inspector. He nodded.

'Wow!' Beth said at last under her breath.

The moment passed. Suddenly, everyone wanted to talk at the same time.

'It's a powerful motive,' I said. 'It doesn't prove that either of them killed him.'

'Of course not,' Ewell said. 'Whenever you get a miscarriage of justice it's because a motive has been mistaken for real evidence. But it gives us what we badly needed, a new direction. It gives us grounds for enquiry. We applied for a search warrant but it was turned down. Sir Ian Bewlay has a lot of clout and some powerful friends. What goes for him goes for Mr Pratt too. With this, we can move ahead.'

'So it was all right to search our house,' Beth said scathingly, 'but not the houses of those two pompous . . .' Her voice tailed away for lack of the *mot juste*.

Hannah furnished it. 'Arseholes,' she said, amazing herself as well as the rest of us. She covered her mouth. I guessed that she had spoken from the heart.

'That's not a nice way to speak about anybody,' Beth warned. 'But you're close,' she added.

'There was a direct and immediate connection between you and Mr Webb,' said Ewell, reverting to where our discussion had been side-tracked. 'His only connection with Sir Ian and Mr Pratt was that each admitted to having sold him something at a bargain price, some time in the past.'

Beth was ready with a sharp answer, but I had had enough. 'We have a business to run,' I said. And, as we moved towards the door, I added, 'You should be able to manage without us now.' It was unfair of me, perhaps, but I had had a bellyful of the police and it would have taken a more angelic man than me not to crow, just a little.

Chapter Twelve

For several days, nothing whatever was to be learned except for guarded statements from the police to the media that they were following up a fresh line of enquiry and that an arrest was expected daily. It was the statement which comes off the rubber stamp during every murder case, but this time we knew that it could be true.

Then a letter arrived for Hannah from a solicitor. True to his type, Dougal Webb had never got around to taking out an insurance policy, which would have cost him serious money. But he had made out a valid will, using a will form from the Post Office, and had deposited it with the solicitor named as his executor. He had kept his word and left his car to Hannah along with a modest legacy in cash. So, eventually, the Lotus came to lend a little class to our gravel and Hannah, who had been taught to drive in our car by Daffy but had never before driven anything much faster than a bicycle, began collecting speeding tickets as though they were trading stamps and motor-minded boy-friends as though they were given away with a pound of tea.

Detective Inspector Ewell called to see us while we were still agog at the news of Hannah's good fortune. He was accompanied by Detective Sergeant Bremner, who seemed strangely unwilling to make eye contact with any of us. They accepted tea in the sitting room with Hannah and Beth and me.

'This is in confidence for another day or two,' Ewell said. 'But we know fine that you can keep a confidence and you've never been noted for talking to the press. We owe it to you to let you know how it worked out. The signs are that it's all over.'

'You got your search warrant, then?' Beth said.

'With that videotape, there was no doubt of it. And it paid off handsomely. I'll let Sergeant Bremner tell you about it.'

He looked benignly at the Sergeant, who flushed. I realized suddenly that this visit was no mere courtesy but was intended to rub the Sergeant's delicate nose in the mess that had been in the making.

'Blood was found between the tiles in the kitchen at Marksmuir House and also in Sir Ian's vehicle,' said the Sergeant. She spoke woodenly and if her teeth were not gritted they were very close to it. 'The same blood group as Mr Webb and we're in no doubt that it will prove to have been his when the DNA tests are finished. Fibres found in Webb's car match the cloth of Mr Pratt's coat. An examination of some disturbed ground resulted in the unearthing of a knife-handle belonging to the blade found in Mr Webb's body.'

She paused. 'Go on,' said Ewell. The Sergeant sighed.

225

'Sir Ian and Mr Pratt made formal statements after cautioning. Each was adamant that he had not been on Gifford Hill for years or, in Mr Pratt's case, ever. But the soil, seeds and pollen on Gifford Hill are a unique mix and we have a soil scientist prepared to prove in court that that's where the dirt we found in the welts of Mr Pratt's shoes and Sir Ian's shooting boots came from.

'Faced with this evidence, each changed his story and tried to blame the other. Between the two versions, we can put together the truth. Mr Webb came up to Marksmuir House. It was Sunday, the housekeeper's day off, and the two men were catering for themselves in the kitchen. Webb said that he had the videotape. He then offered to buy Mr Pratt's camcorder and Sir Ian's big four-by-four, for sums which we can assume were paltry. Both men had been bitten once before. Tempers flared. What was being asked from Mr Pratt was the lesser demand, but he was less able than Sir Ian to foot the bill.'

'If he'd paused for a moment,' said Detective Inspector Ewell, 'he might have realized that the video-tape would be far more damaging to Sir Ian, who could well have afforded to foot both bills. In fact, Mr Pratt's only sin had been to distribute the tape showing his own heroism and suppress that part showing Sir Ian's appalling carelessness. But Pratt realized that if his patron was knocked off his pedestal he too would suffer. He became furious and struck the fatal blow. We know it from the spots of blood on the sleeve of his coat. Go on, Sergeant.'

'When they realized that Webb was dead,' Sergeant Bremner resumed, 'they put the body in Sir Ian's car, the one that Webb fancied so much, and scrubbed out the kitchen. Around one in the morning, they went out together, Sir Ian conveying the body and Mr Pratt driving Mr Webb's Lotus. They left the Lotus at Cupar station, then drove to Gifford Hill and carried the body up to the bonfire site.'

'And they broke into Dougal Webb's cottage hoping to recover the tape,' I said.

Ewell nodded. 'Probably both of them, but we're sure of Sir Ian. We already had a fingerprint which now proves to be his.' The Detective Inspector got to his feet, so the Sergeant followed suit. 'I felt that we owed you a word of thanks,' he said briskly, 'and also an apology. I'm afraid that we gave you a hard time.'

'None of your doing, I'm sure, Mr Ewell,' Beth said.

I glanced at the Sergeant. She looked as though she had bitten into a wormy apple. The Inspector had noted it too but he was merciless. 'We're very grateful,' he said warmly.

'And no doubt you've had pats on the back from upstairs,' I suggested.

He managed a faint smile. 'Some of us have,' he said. 'Come, Sergeant.'

When the case came to the High Court, it was over almost before it had begun. In the eyes of the jury, the evidence was conclusive. Defence counsel struggled to argue that blackmailers were fair game and in season, but the fact that money, however little, had been offered rather than demanded rather clouded the issue with the jury. Pratt, the dealer of the blow, was sent to where he would have a captive audience for his pontificating. Sir Ian, as an accomplice after the fact, received a lesser sentence; but his ambitions were in tatters and he was disgraced.

In the meantime, more events had overtaken some of the other participants.

A second case was dealt with in a lower court by the sheriff. Mrs Macevoy was charged with harbouring a prisoner on the run, or some such wording. Her plea that she went in terror of her husband and had acted under duress held little water, since she had continued to deny his presence until the moment the officers lifted the hatch in the floor, but it must have had some effect with the judge because she was treated leniently. She was sentenced to do a hundred hours of Community Service, ministering to the residents in a home for the elderly and the mentally handicapped. It was generally believed that she would much rather have gone to prison.

When he went back to his ship, Jimmy Dundee left his mother better provided for. He also gave her a wad of tickets in the National Lottery and only a month later one of them brought her a one-third share in a roll-over jackpot. She continues to live quite happily in her cottage, but as soon as it became clear that Sir Ian would never return to Fife she bought Marksmuir Estate for a price which must have had the thrifty gentleman grinding his teeth. But long-standing habits are hard to break. Every afternoon she spends at work in the big house, although her Jimmy has left the sea and now, as well as living in the house, runs a business in garden supplies from the gardens and outbuildings. He is often to be seen with Hannah, driving the Lotus at a rather more sober pace than hers.

Quentin Cove's misdeeds were never brought home to him, except that Rex paid him a visit after which the two men, both somewhat battered, adjourned to the nearest pub and got drunk together. Daffy never quite forgave Quentin for the death of Mim, but we never found another supply of dog-food as good and as convenient as his and with Daffy's agreement we became his customers again. When Hebe produced another throwback to Champion Clunie of Netherbrae, Quentin was on the doorstep long before the pup was weaned, brandishing a fistful of twenty-pound notes. The two get on well together. So far, he has not managed to make her up to Champion, but at least having a goal is good for him.

Quentin has one other ambition. He would dearly love to add the Marksmuir land to Ardrossie and with that in mind pays court to Elsie Dundee. But he does not have it all his own way. Jack Gilchrist, among others, is a rival for her hand. She has not been such an object of desire since Sir Ian first tumbled her on the dining room table.

Mrs Dundee and her son have never forgotten what little help I was able to give them. Or perhaps they think that they are buying my silence. But the sporting rights to Marksmuir land are let to me for a peppercorn rent. And that is what I call a happy ending.